JUST THIEVES

ALSO BY GREGORY GALLOWAY

As Simple as Snow
The 39 Deaths of Adam Strand

GREGORY
GALLOWAY

Just Thieves

First Melville House Printing: August 2021

Melville House Publishing
46 John Street
Brooklyn, NY 11201
and
Melville House UK
Suite 2000
16/18 Woodford Road
London E7 0HA

mhpbooks.com
@melvillehouse

ISBN: 978-1-61219-937-5
ISBN: 978-1- 61219-938-2 (eBook)

Library of Congress Control Number: 2021942131

Designed by Amy C. King

Printed in the United States of America
10 9 8 7 6 5 4 3 2 1
A catalog record for this book is available from the Library of Congress

FOR MICHAEL

(1959–2018)

IIIII

“In times of terror, when everyone is something of a conspirator, everyone will be in a situation where he has to play detective.”

WALTER BENJAMIN

“The criminal is the creative artist.”

G. K. CHESTERTON

1
THE HORSE

WE DIDN'T KNOW HOW IT HAPPENED, BUT WHEN WE WOKE UP THERE WAS A DEAD HORSE IN THE STREET IN FRONT OF THE HOTEL. The sun wasn't up but it was light out, that part of the day I like best, not quite day but no longer night. It feels like the start of something. You can go out and see the world and not be bothered. Usually. But now there was a large dead animal in the street, and a small crowd, five or six people with nothing better to do than stand around and take pictures. "Don't look at it," I told Frank, knowing he wouldn't listen. There was no saddle, no bridle, and no blood, nothing but a large gray horse dead in the middle of the road. It must have just happened too; there wasn't a cop or fireman, or any official-looking person around to deal with a corpse in the street. Just people like us, headed out for the day with things to do, never expecting to have a dead horse literally thrown right in our way.

We were supposed to be on our way to work, but this would change things, alter the entire day, if I knew Frank. He'd have to think about it. He'd have to think about it a lot. We should have stayed there, in the street with the horse, maybe, in retrospect, so he could take a good look at everything. Let him take it all in and work it all out right there. That's what we should have done. Maybe the whole day would have gone different; maybe the whole thing. In the moment, though, I thought the sooner I got Frank away from the horse, the sooner he'd stop thinking about it. It wasn't the first time I've been wrong like this. "Let's go," I said and Frank didn't seem to want to stay anyway, so we walked into the nearest diner and took a booth in the back.

At times like this, Frank tended to see omens in the smallest accidents. He wasn't exactly a superstitious sort, not the black-cat, broken-mirror, bad-luck type. He was worse than that in a way. He thought the world operated with an efficient underlying malevolency; it all operated according to a specific set of rules, and if you paid close enough attention you could avoid its damage. He didn't believe in surprises or coincidences, each event was a gear in a large machine that rolled on and on, rewarding those who paid attention to its inner workings, and punishing those who ignored them. Once, when we were on a job not unlike this one, we were getting ready to go out in the middle of the night, when the hotel's emergency lights began flashing and alarms sounded in every hallway. Frank wanted to stop right there and get back into bed. He refused to leave the room. He didn't want me to leave either. I went anyway. We had a job to do. The elevators weren't working and I had to walk down eight flights of stairs. There was a man in a wheelchair on the seventh-floor landing and he asked if I would help him.

"I can't do it by myself," I said. He was a big guy. "You can't leave me here," the guy said. So I stood and waited for a stranger to come along. Our good intentions were quickly overtaken by our incompetence. We struggled with every stair, negotiating the man and the chair carefully down and down, the uncooperative weight of him getting worse and worse every floor, while he complained every inch of the way.

IIIII

"Watch it," he'd say, convinced he was going to tip, but we had him. Unfortunately we had him. "What are you stopping for," he said as we caught our breath on the fourth-floor landing. We looked like death, me and the stranger, in the harsh emergency light, and the pulsing of the alarms only made everything worse. My ears were ringing and my heart was pounding against my chest like it was trapped and I thought I should be the one in the wheelchair. But we went back to work and got the guy down. By the time we reached the ground level, the lights were back on and everyone was headed back to their rooms. The guy in the wheelchair was pissed off. At us.

"You should have left me up there," he said. "I knew it was nothing."

I wandered off without saying a word. I went back to the room and didn't tell Frank anything about the wheelchair. He didn't need to know about that gear of his machine. "The whole block was out," I told him. "Twenty minutes, tops." It went out again, flickered then went black before the emergency lights kicked on and the alarms sounded again. We went back to bed. The job had to wait. Frank could wait, wait for the gears to move smoothly again.

"We're engaged in criminal activity," Frank liked to argue in regard to his superstitions. "Criminals get caught because they don't pay attention, don't plan enough, don't see the problems until it's too late. I don't want surprises. We need to avoid them." That's why I put up with him. Besides, you couldn't argue with our success. We'd never been caught. But then Frank had luck on his side, more than he'd ever admit.

We were thieves. We stole anything, paintings, cars, coins, guns, houseplants, it didn't matter. We stole a pair of sneakers (only twenty-three ever made, Frank said); they were just around the guy's closet, tangled with slippers and flip-flops. "The rich always get what they want," Frank said afterward, "but they usually don't want it once they get it." That's where we come in.

We never stole anything for ourselves. It was all strictly by request. A guy said, "I need this," and we went and got it. We were small-timers with small jobs. I'd been doing it for a while before I met Frank, but business was better once he joined. I knew what I was doing, but Frank had an expertise in things. Plus, Frank had a good face for it. Good-looking without standing out. He had a calm, friendly way about him. Pleasant. People wanted to like him. Frank could walk into a bakery and walk out with twenty loaves, unnoticed. He could stand across the street from our target and no one would think twice. "I'm going to rob that house tonight," he could have told them and they'd nod and say, "That's nice." Because of his face, and the way he had about him. People trusted him. I trusted him for a long time.

People look but they don't see. You can have twelve people looking at the dead horse in the street and ten will give you ten different descriptions of the same thing. And the two people who agree are most likely to have it all wrong. One thing I've learned is that if someone is staring at you, you've got nothing to worry about. They're fixated on one thing, your hair or your nose, maybe a freckle on your ear - who the hell knows - but they're not seeing you, they're only seeing some small part, and when they have to recall the whole person, they can't. More times than not, they can't even accurately remember the thing they were staring at.

I let them stare. Or if I think they're doing more than looking, actually taking notice of what I look like, then I stare back. Look right at them. They almost always look away, and the minute they look away, they stop remembering. It all goes away, or gets changed around in their minds.

I have a bland face anyway. Tough to remember, harder to describe. Not good-looking at all, but not so bad. Indistinguishable. That was my gift. No one could describe me with any accuracy. I'm fortunate with youthful features, and a mobility of expression which baffles all observers and provides a great strength and chief safeguard. By what signs can one hope to identify a face which changes at pleasure, even without the help of makeup, and whose every transient expression seems to be the final, definite expression? People can never remember what I look like. I was even questioned once an hour after stealing a woman's jewelry - she'd gotten a good look at me and then standing right in front of me at the police station she didn't recognize me. By the time the cops had found me, I'd already ditched the stuff, so I stood there and let her look. "It's not him," the woman said, and I was free to go.

I go through life as I please and no one pays me any mind. That's a good life, as long as it lasts.

IIIII

Frank had a cup of coffee, then he had another one, without saying anything. It wasn't good. He could sit like that all day. He was like a chess player who looks at the board and figures out how every piece got where it was, looks at the board for as long as it takes, with the clock spinning hurriedly beside him, then figures out how to move from there. Frank would think about the horse and the people who were out on the street when we arrived, and then he'd try to figure out where they came from, what they were doing, where they were going, and why. There was no point in telling him that it had nothing to do with us. We saw it, were part of it, Frank would say, so of course it has something to do with us.

But what does it have to do with us? That's what Frank had to figure out. He'd get there, I knew he would, but it could be a while. It was times like this I wished I still drank. Or smoked. Anything to pass the time while Frank figured it out. Until then we were both stuck. Frank drank his coffee and I watched him, trying to stay out of his way as long as possible. But we didn't have all day.

"We had a plan."

I knew it was a mistake the minute I said it.

"Every day starts with a plan," Frank said, "and then it all goes out the window. We think it's going to behave according to the way we want it, according to our plans, but why should it? Why should we be surprised that there are a lot more things going on in the world than the things we want out of it?"

"We've done all right."

"We have. Which is amazing, isn't it? Failure should outweigh success, that's the way the world has to work. You know that. You see that. Just look at today. Most days are nothing more than barely contained accidents."

On a different day I would have argued with him. I would have told him that it's not the accident that's important, it's the reaction to the accident. You can't let it affect everything; you can't let it derail everything. I know what he would say; he'd said it many times before. "Everybody thinks they're in control, but there are forces in the world that control us. All we can do is try to navigate through those forces."

He had another saying that I liked, but didn't necessarily agree with. "Everybody's autobiography should be told in the passive voice," he said. "Our lives are shaped more by things we can't control than those we can. We are worked on by the world, not the other way around. All we can do is react." Frank was reacting to it the best way anyone could. He was recalculating everything, working to get us back on track. I let him work.

He went back to his coffee and thinking about the horse and how the world took apart our plans as if they were nothing, which they were, of course. Frank knew the way the world worked, more than most, which is why I stayed with him, which is why I was sitting in a diner staring at a cup of coffee when we should be out working, when were expected to be out working. I knew we'd have to answer for it. I'd have to answer for it. Frank never dealt with that side of things. This made me impatient. That's what Frank tolerated, but he wouldn't give in.

"So what do you want to do, Frank?"

"That was a cop's horse," he said.

"Could be from one of those carriages. Could be anything. We don't know these things."

"It's not good," he said. "Somebody should have been with him, not just left him in the street like that. It's not good."

"What do you want to do?"

Frank had another cup of coffee, but not another word. I sat and waited for him. What else was I going to do? I couldn't do anything without him.

We'd been hired to come and grab something. We got a call from my usual guy, Froehmer, who gave us an address or the name of the guy and then what we should take from him. It's easy, Froehmer said, the way they always do. If it's so easy, I said, then you don't need us.

I'd done a lot of work with Froehmer. He'd helped me out when I needed it, back when I was just starting out. Froehmer didn't pay well, but he always had work. Everything was easy for him. For as long as I'd known him, it was all easy for him. I had to remind him that it wasn't so easy for the rest of us. He didn't mind. Just get it done, he said. Don't wait more than a couple of days. The item might be on the move.

So we drove all the way here and got our room. We didn't know anyone, weren't supposed to do anything except find the guy and take

what we came for. We couldn't even do that. Frank wouldn't do anything now, not until he figured out the horse. The day had started out one way and now here we were wasting time while Frank figured on the dead horse. It wasn't a sign; he didn't think that way. Frank was a smart guy, maybe the smartest guy I knew, but that was part of the trouble. He could think himself into things that weren't necessarily so. Maybe it was a cop's horse, so what? It doesn't mean the cop knew anything about us. But the cops will be all over the street outside the hotel, Frank argued. Maybe they'll want to talk to everybody around, talk to us. We'll check out then. Move to a different place. That's the worst thing we could do, Frank said.

"So what do you want to do?"

IIIII

Maybe I started this the wrong way. You might have the wrong idea about Frank and me. I have no complaints with him, in fact, just the opposite. I wouldn't be where I am without Frank, wouldn't have anything if it wasn't for him. He has his faults and eccentricities, but fewer than most, really. He's made his share of mistakes, but made fewer than I have, and has kept me from making plenty more. He brings more to the job than I do and doesn't expect more of me than I can give. What more can you ask from someone?

Frank's a thinker, by nature and by choice. He can sit and think through about anything, taking it apart and putting it back together in his mind until he's got it all figured out. It has helped us get at stuff no one thought we could. He could pull off one of those heists you see in the movies, complicated jobs that require all sorts of knowledge and planning and perfect timing and only work in the movies. I'm sure he could do it. He doesn't want to. Leave it alone, he says. "If it's that much effort, it's too much trouble." Frank could sit at home and steal stuff

from all over the world if he wanted. He can figure out most hacks. I've seen him break into banks and corporations and government sites. He did it just to see how it was done, but it doesn't interest us, not as an occupation. We like the small stuff, get into a house, an office, someplace you walk into and out of, not running your fingers over a bunch of keys. Where's the fun in that? Frank would rather do the jobs we do, grab and go. He doesn't want much, and he doesn't need much. We get by all right and he never complains. I get the work and we do it and that's all there is to it.

IIIII

I loved him, I suppose. He drove me crazy enough. We'd been partners for a while, knew how to work together. That was the important thing. I didn't have any secrets with him. Well, fewer than most.

2

THE HOTEL

WE LEFT THE DINER AND WENT BACK TO THE HOTEL. The horse was gone and people went along the street as if it had never been there, as if none of it had happened. We began to think it hadn't.

"What happened to the horse?" I said to the woman behind the counter in the lobby.

She was the same woman who was working when we'd left, but she acted as if she'd never seen us before, and didn't know what we were talking about. "Horse?"

"There was a horse outside in the street this morning."

"A horse?"

The phone rang and she answered it. Frank and I went to the elevator. "She thinks we're crazy and we think she's crazy," Frank said. "All from one word."

"Horse?" I said, with a good imitation of her tone and uptalk at the end of the syllable. At least it got Frank to laugh for a moment, but then he went back to thinking. The way he does.

The elevator lifted us hundreds of feet in the air, quietly and assuredly, and Frank studied the buttons in the small metal box as if they were a complicated code that needed to be deciphered. "Everybody knows the story of the experimental philosopher who had a great theory about a horse being able to live without eating," Frank said, not to me as much as to the buttons in front of him, "and who demonstrated it so well, that he had got his own horse down to a straw a day, and would unquestionably have rendered him a very spirited and rampacious animal on nothing at all, if the horse had not died, just twenty-four hours before he was to have had his first comfortable bit of air." The doors opened on our floor and I stepped out of the elevator, but not before noticing that Frank had pressed the button for the lobby. He didn't say anything; I didn't say anything. I would go to the room. Frank would go back to the horseless street.

I sat in the almost life-size armchair in the room and took a scrap of paper out of my pocket and looked at the penciled address on it. It's where we were supposed to be. That had been our destination in the morning, and should be our destination now. I shouldn't be sitting in a hotel room staring at an address; I should be at the address staring at the house it belonged to. We'd never had trouble with that part of the plan before. I wasn't sure how to explain it to Froehmer. I was still hoping I wouldn't have to explain it.

We had checked into the hotel the night before. We'd done a few jobs for Froehmer outside of town, but never this far. We drove down and parked in a public lot and walked to the hotel and waited for a line to form at reception, then checked in and went to the room. They hardly ever notice you when you're at the counter, anyway. They say your name a few times and glance at you, but they hardly ever notice. You could ask them a few seconds after you leave to describe you and name you, and they couldn't. They've already dumped that information and are on to the next. Still, we try to be as invisible as possible. We never order room service, rarely talk to anyone else in the hotel, and avoid the lobby and public places as much as possible. We take precautions, almost all of them unnecessary, but we take them anyway. "Luck is when opportunity meets preparation," Frank had said, quoting another fortune cookie. I had that one in my pocket for a while. I fished around in my jacket and found one. "For success today, look first to yourself."

I took the elevator back to the lobby and walked out onto the street. Frank was nowhere around. I walked toward the car and passing a garbage bin, threw the fortune away.

IIIII

I sat in the backseat of the rental car, more obscured by the tinted windows, and picked at a carton of takeout and took a look at the target property. It's what I hated about the job, one of the main reasons I worked with Frank and not alone. It's boring. You sit for a day or two and watch. You watch who comes and goes and when, how long they are gone, what do they do when they leave. Sometimes we might follow them. Sometimes we just sit for hours and hours and look. Frank, almost always Frank, takes a look at any alarms or surveillance systems. He takes a look at the network, wi-fi, whatever, anything that might be used to monitor the place. Nine times out of ten there's nothing complicated.

People get lazy. Some people lock their windows and leave a door open. People who have a security system they operate with their phone are locking the door while leaving the windows alone. It's easy. We don't do much of that. We're not burglars, we're thieves. But we do what we have to. The chances of someone being robbed are about twenty-six in a thousand. Not very likely. So people get lazy. They stop turning on their alarms; they don't fix them once they break; they don't renew their contract with a security company; they stop locking all doors and windows. They live their life without worry and nothing happens so they get comfortable and happier and lazier, and all we have to do is sit and wait. We're a little lazy ourselves; we don't want a challenge, just a quick grab and go. You'd be surprised how well it works. "There's a guy in France who stole five paintings worth more than one hundred million dollars," Frank told me one night as we waited in the car. "All he used was a pair of pliers, a screwdriver, a knife, and a couple of plungers. Stole it all from the same museum on the same night. Braque, Picasso, Léger, Matisse, and Modigliani. All with a handful of tools and a little smarts. That's all it takes."

"That's all it takes."

IIIII

I texted Frank. "At the place." I fished around in the take-out bag and found the fortune cookie. "Today's cookie," I texted again. "Not all closed eyes are sleeping. Not all open eyes are seeing." He didn't respond. Maybe he thought it was funny. I threw everything back in the bag and went back to looking at the place. It was a quiet street, not a lot of activity during the daytime. I took a walk around and got close to the place, looked at a few windows and doors, then sat in the car for a few more hours. I almost fell asleep a couple of times it was so boring. I wasn't cut out for doing this on my own anymore. When I was younger I liked being by myself. But Froehmer didn't have me doing this type of stuff then. None of the early work took much planning, but it was all higher risk. This was low risk if you did your homework, had a good plan, and followed the plan. This wasn't going to take much. The family had a nice place, not a whole lot of valuable stuff laying around, and lived in a safe, comfortable neighborhood. They didn't have anything to worry about.

A young boy came home first, high schooler, head down in his phone, not paying attention to anything other than the small screen in front of him. A woman came home about an hour and half later, then a man about a half hour after that. It all looked the way you'd expect. I took notice of the times and watched a while longer. We could stay on schedule. I could tell Froehmer that everything was going to be all right. He'd get what he wanted right on schedule. We didn't even know what it was yet. That's how it usually worked. We figured out how to get the thing, then once we had a plan, Froehmer told us what it was. Once in a while, we had to know what it was beforehand, if it was too big or bulky or whatever, but usually we didn't know what the thing was until the last second. That was the one part Frank wasn't too crazy about, but it was that way from the start. It had all worked out all right for us so far.

Frank liked to know what it was we were taking so he could figure out how much it was worth. He didn't care, but he always liked to know. You'd be surprised at how much junk is worth. I mean, some of the ugliest, unlikeliest things are worth more than you'd ever imagine. We took this horrible piece of pottery one time, that we were convinced wasn't worth our time that ended up being worth almost twenty thousand. Over the years, however, Frank's gotten good at telling the minute we see something.

"You ever wonder where it goes?" Frank once asked me.

"It goes to Froehmer," I said.

We actually stole an item twice. Froehmer had hired us to take a painting one time, then about three years later he had us go someplace else for a painting. It was the same one. We didn't say anything; we figured Froehmer knew. We figured that was his business. Somebody wanted something rare or whatever and asked Froehmer to find it for them and paid him for it. Frank and I figured that must be what Froehmer's role was. He located the stuff, told us the location, and we gave the stuff to Froehmer. We got paid by the job and Froehmer probably got a fee based on the value of the thing. It probably wasn't fair, but we didn't care. We really didn't. We did all right, Frank and I. I could have made more money working on my own, but I didn't want to do that. And now that I'd worked with Frank for so long, I couldn't stand to be alone. I watched the place a while longer, then drove back to the hotel.

Frank was sitting in the almost life-size chair when I got back to the room. "We got nothing to worry about," I told him. "We can get this whenever you're ready. I can do it by myself, if you're not up for it."

"I'm ready," Frank said. "But you should have waited."

"I know. But Froehmer has a deadline."

"What good is a deadline if we get caught."

"We're not going to get caught," I said. "I told you. There's nothing to worry about."

"There was," he said, meaning the horse.

"You figured it out?"

"I think so," he said and then didn't say anything else. I gave him that. Let him keep it for a while. I didn't really care. Not that much, anyway.

IIIII

Frank was better suited to this life than I am, something I didn't discover until after he joined me. He had the right temperament for sitting for hours, and he knew when to be quiet and when to break the silence. He would sit and think, his mind off somewhere, and he'd forget that mine wasn't in the same place and he'd say something that might take me a minute to catch on to how he got there. "Anything but blind," Frank said, continuing a conversation he'd been having silently with himself. I knew what he was saying. That would be the worst, I told him.

"I wouldn't mind not seeing stuff," Frank said, "but I couldn't stand not knowing where I was or who was around. I'd think the walls were closing in or someone was out to get me."

"Someone's always out to get you, Frank."

|||||

I wanted to go home. The thought woke me up, I think. Or maybe I was awake already, and only startled by the thought. I'd never thought that way before, but there I was in the dark hotel room, all of a sudden thinking I wanted to leave. The darkness of the room seemed too close, unnaturally close. Frank was asleep; the whole building was asleep for all I knew, every room and every guest, and the dark decided to move in on me and make me want to flee, for the first time. I stared at the ceiling and tried to think my way out of it. Another day; another night at the most and we'd be done and gone, back home and back to Froehmer and it would all be behind us. There was nothing to worry about with this job. Frank would see for himself tomorrow and I'd be in and out in less than a minute or so and everything would be fine. I could see it all, the way into the house, the room, the shelf, the item, me taking it and going right back out. Everything would go exactly as I saw it in my mind; everything would go exactly as it had every other time, with no problem. Frank had figured out his dead horse and I had this figured out. It was only a passing thought in my head, wanting to leave. There was nothing to worry about. It was only dark. And Froehmer was out there waiting. Froehmer was waiting for us to deliver. We wouldn't disappoint.

3

FROEHMER

I WAS TOLD TO MEET HIM AT THE DINER. I was nineteen, barely out of high school and didn't have a clue to what I was doing. All I knew was that I needed help. I was told he could help. He was a friend of my father's. Froehmer. I'd known him most of my life. Growing up, he'd come around the house to see my father all the time, but I hadn't seen him in years. I wasn't sure I would even know him now. I had enough other shit on my mind. My father arranged the meeting and told me to wait for him. So I waited. And waited. I'd ordered some soup and thirty-five minutes later it was cold and I was still waiting. I'd never waited thirty minutes for anything, never in my life. The waitress came and took away the soup and then came back and took my money. I still waited. Then my phone rang.

"Where are you?" Froehmer said.

"I'm where I'm supposed to be."

"I'm at the fucking diner. Where the fuck are you?"

"I've been waiting right here."

"Where? Never mind, I see you."

I put the phone back in my pocket and a guy almost three times my age moved toward me with a cup of coffee in one hand and his other hand clenched in a fist I half-thought he might throw any second. I stood up and put out my hand, but he ignored me and slid into the booth on the other side. I didn't recognize him at all. It had been too long, long enough for him to get old. I had a younger man in my head, in good shape, somebody who'd played a sport in college, lacrosse probably, squash, one of those club sports that don't count for anything, I thought. He looked like that kind of guy to me, back in the day. Now he was gray, sagging a bit here and there. I saw the younger version of him in the folds and wrinkles, but it took me a minute.

"You forget who I am?" Froehmer said.

"No."

"You should have found me. Not the other way around."

"I didn't see you, I guess. I was here at eleven, just like you said."

"I've been here thirty years," he said, "waiting on guys just like you. Only I don't wait. Usually."

I took a sip of water, even though the glass was empty.

"You should order something," he said. "How's your dad?"

"Trying to stay positive."

"What's he have to do now, three times a week?"

I nodded. "Three times a week. And that's the way it's going to be, I guess."

"Good doctors?"

"Real good."

“Your dad’s a good man,” he said.

“He says the very same about you.”

The waitress came and I ordered a burger. Froehmer didn’t want anything, which made me think I shouldn’t have ordered. He knew what he was doing, I thought; and I didn’t have a clue.

“Your father said you had a question.”

“I could use some help,” I said. “My girlfriend had a kid about a year ago, you know. Now she’s with somebody else, somebody I don’t want around the kid, so I’m wondering what that would take. You know, to keep the guy away from my kid?”

“Who’s the guy?”

“I don’t know him.”

“You know a name.”

“I don’t even know what he looks like,” I said. “I’ve never seen him. But I know he’s no good. No good for the kid, no good for anybody.”

“Cause he’s with your girlfriend?”

“It’s not that,” I said. “I don’t care about the ex. I care about my kid. The guys got a drug problem. I don’t want him around the kid.”

“They sure drop the net over you, don’t they?” Froehmer said. “How about the ex? She using?”

“I think so, but not like him.”

“What have you done about it?”

“I got that restraining order over me.”

“That’s what your dad said.”

“He’s not happy about it.”

“Are you?”

I shrugged. “I should have called you first.”

“It would have been cheaper, in the long run.”

“What do you think it will take?”

“You want him moved off, or just moved back?”

"Back, I guess. I don't care what she does. How much?"

"More than you'll want, but I'll have to talk to some people. We'll look into it."

"Somebody said he's got a reputation as a hard-ass or something. He won't be easy."

Froehmer shrugged. "You never know. We'll see how it goes."

The waitress came and put down a plate with a hamburger and a large pile of fries and a bright green spear of pickle.

"How's work?"

I laughed and then regretted it. "I haven't worked in almost six months. Nobody's building, so nobody's hiring."

"You want to work?"

"That would be great, if it's no trouble."

Froehmer looked at my plate and nodded. "I'll talk to some people."

"My dad says you could talk Christ off the cross."

"I'm not sure that would do anyone any good."

"What happens now?"

"I talk to some people, then they talk to some people, then they talk to me and I talk to you."

"That's it?"

"That's it."

"And it will cost me."

"I'll let you know. It's going to be fair, but I'll let you know. You don't have to do anything."

"I want it done, but I'm not working and all."

"Okay."

"You can't give me an idea now?"

"It's not about the idea. It's not about the number. It's about what you want. You want the kid safe? How much is that worth? What's the number you'd put up for that? You want to do it cheap, do it yourself. You know where that would get you. This way it's done right and you don't have to worry. All we did was talk. Everything else gets done right and you get what you want. You get that idea, right?"

"Okay."

"Okay."

I looked down at the plate. Everything was gone except smears of ketchup. The waitress placed the bill face down on the table. "I would have got yours," I said.

"I took care of it," Froehmer said.

We stood up and left and Froehmer walked for a few steps into the parking lot.

"Don't call me," Froehmer said. "You'll hear from me soon. If you don't, don't call me. But you'll hear. This is nothing to worry about."

"You should come see my father. He'd like that."

"I'd like that too," Froehmer said. He wouldn't go see him. Three times a week. Who wants to see that? He hadn't seen him in a long time, before he was sick. It was better to leave it like that. Three times a week, hooked up to a machine, is that how he'd want to be remembered? "Tell him I'll come by soon."

IIIII

I'd been working for Froehmer for a couple of months, paying back what I owed him. He had me stealing stuff from construction sites around town, tools, equipment, material, whatever he told me. Then he called me and wanted to meet back at the diner, but we didn't go in. We sat in his car, which is always a bad sign, right?

"You think you could get something for me?" he said.

"Sure."

"It's an inside job. You'd have to get into some guy's house," he said.

"Tell me what it is and I'll get it for you."

He wrote down an address with a pencil on a scrap of paper and handed it to me.

"Pieces of silver," he said.

I thought he was joking but I didn't laugh.

"It's in the guy's office, in his house," Froehmer said. "They're in a wooden box, about the size of a pencil case. It'll be on his desk or in it, or on his bookcase, some place like that. It's a wooden box. Make sure the coins are in it. You'll know the box when you see it. It's an easy job."

"What if it's in a safe or something?" I said, immediately regretting saying anything.

"It's on the desk or bookcase," Froehmer said. He wasn't going to say anything else, but then thought better of it. "People are lazy," he said, "but the rich are really lazy. Or careless. Or both."

I guess it makes sense. If you had five dollars and one good watch, you guard them with your life, but if you had 5 million and 50 watches, maybe you don't care about five dollars and one watch, maybe you can't keep track of it all, anyway. I nodded at Froehmer and hoped he'd still give me a chance.

"If it's not in the office, don't look for it, just get out and let me know."

"When do you want it?"

"Friday," he said.

That gave me a couple of days to figure out what I was doing.

Stealing is instinctual. Everyone (and I mean everyone) does it; robbery is a skill; and thievery is a science. I knew I had to study, so I went to the address and looked around, then went back and watched, studied the house and the people who lived in it. I saw the office and the guy who had the thing Froehmer wanted. I watched myself and made sure no one noticed me. I knew what I was doing, I told myself. I knew I had the right instincts; I wasn't sure that I had the right talent.

IIIII

There was a window open in the back, and a screen that could be pushed out of its frame. I was standing in the office in seconds. The dark oak desk, looked like a monument, and seemed to take up most of the room. I stood behind the leather chair and looked at it. I had time. There were two books on the desk, *Labor and Organization in Crisis*, and *The Study of Economic Cycles*, nothing of interest. There were a series of framed photos I didn't bother to notice, an antique lamp (or reproduction), a couple of stacks of papers, a paperweight with a gold piece in the center, and a small wooden box exactly like Froehmer had described. I opened it to make sure the silver coins were inside, then put it in my shoulder bag and went out the way I had come. I hadn't touched anything I shouldn't have, hadn't disturbed anything, even put the screen back in the window when I left. There was nothing to worry about. I worried anyway. I worried all night and all the next day and the day after that, as long as I had possession of the thing, until finally Froehmer arranged a meeting and I handed it to the man Froehmer had sent. I didn't like that part of it. I didn't know the man. I only knew Froehmer. And now both of them knew what I'd done.

"How's the kid?" Froehmer said one day, not long after he'd got his silver.

"Good," I said. Froehmer probably knew I hadn't seen the kid. He probably knew more about it than I did.

"You've worked it off, in case you were wondering." I wasn't. Froehmer had given me cash enough to live off of, and deducted the other, I guess.

"That's good news."

"So you can go on working the way you've been doing, or we can make other arrangements, or you can go on and do whatever you want."

"Okay."

"Think about it."

"I'll do whatever you need," I said.

"You've got an aptitude," Froehmer said. "We could take advantage of that, put that to use, the way you've been. Keep you off construction sites if you want."

"Okay."

"The pay's better. If that's okay."

"That's okay by me."

"Okay then," Froehmer said. "We'll be in touch."

I didn't hear from him for almost a week. Then he texted me and we had breakfast at the diner. He handed me a slip of paper with an address on it. "It's small," he said. "Well, a little bigger than a paperweight, but still, something you won't have any trouble with. Go take a look, and when you've got it figured out, I'll let you know what it is."

That's the way it worked. That's the way it always worked. Except sometimes it wasn't Froehmer. There'd be someone else. I didn't know if they worked for Froehmer like me, or if he'd recommended me to somebody else. I didn't care. I did the work and got paid, a job here and there, and enough money to live and enough time to spend with my father on the days he needed.

"How's work?" he liked to ask.

"Good."

"Froehmer's looking after you?"

"He throws work at me, when he's got it."

"Enough to get by?"

"I can't complain," I said.

"He's a good man to know."

"He says the same about you."

"You could do a lot worse." I wasn't sure if he was talking about Froehmer or himself.

"I'm not sure I could do any better." My father didn't say anything, sitting there strapped to a machine, watching his own blood cycle out of his body, travel around a bunch of tubing and back into his body. This went on for four hours, three days a week. My father wasn't the youngest patient in the place, there were kids in there, cases that would break your heart if you thought about it too much, but he was young, too young. He should have done better. Me, I could have done better. I'm sure he thought it. Here I'd gotten myself into trouble before I was out of my teens, and then more trouble, and had to call in a favor with one of his friends to help me out.

"Everybody makes mistakes," he'd told me. "It's not about the mistake; it's what you do about it."

I could have done better. I could do better. I did something for the kid, I told myself. I kept that other guy away. I would do more, I promised myself. Once I got a little more money coming in, I could do more. Maybe I could even go to school, finish up at the community college for a start. I wouldn't have to be doing jobs for Froehmer forever. I could get a better job. I had time. I wanted to tell my father that I had plenty of time, but what was the point of telling him that? He didn't want to hear it, not now.

"Froehmer says he'll come by when he can," I said.

"I gave him a lot of work over the years," my father said. "He hasn't forgotten."

"He hasn't."

"We did all right together. You should have seen us. We stole from Uncle Sam, believe me, but not too much. They would have wasted it anyway. And we did good work; we did a lot of good work. We did more for this town than a lot of people realize. Other people got the credit. You know, you look around at the old statues and monuments and it says right on them, 'presented by the people' of such and such town, 'dedicated by the town of' such and such; it's all about the community. Now you look at the statues and stuff and it doesn't mention the people. It's all 'dedicated by the mayor' or some other politician. As if they did it themselves. We were the ones in this town. We got a lot done. A lot. We did all right for this town, you know. We just did a little better for ourselves." He laughed a little thinking about it. "You should have seen us, son."

"I remember," I said. My father had to rationalize what he took, to feel as if the mayor or the town, somebody owed him more than the salary he got, the health care, the pension. He never denied that he was a thief, but he always made it sound as if he had a right, as if he earned it. I didn't have that problem. There's nothing personal about it for me.

"Tell Froehmer to come by the house," my father said, "like he used to."

"I will."

"You see him more now than I do. He used to come by all the time."

"He'll be by," I said.

Froehmer would come by the house when I was young, come around to the back and he and my father would sit in the kitchen and have a drink and talk. Froehmer would always bring something, a bottle of something, a bag of something, a cake or pie, cheese, always something. And he'd always have something for me too, candy, gum, a deck of cards with a hole drilled all the way through, always something. I knew who he was, but I didn't know him. I didn't know what they talked about. I didn't know why he was there. Froehmer wasn't the only guy that came around to see my father; there was a whole string of them that would come and go, more after my mother died, and Froehmer wasn't the only guy who brought something, but he was the only one to bring something every time, for me. He was part of my father's world; what did I care about it when I was just a kid, eight, nine, ten years old? I knew who he was and was happy to see him, I guess, but I didn't think about it at all.

"You remember when he took us hunting?" my father said.

It wasn't long after my mother died. Froehmer and some of the others were doing what they could to keep my father occupied, a parade of men coming by, always trying to get us out of the house, away from the reminders for a while, I guess. Froehmer arrived one Saturday morning when it was still pitch-black out and we loaded in his car and drove out to the woods somewhere. It was far. I fell asleep on the way. I was eight, and probably shouldn't have even been on the trip. They didn't give me a gun. The three of us sat in a deer stand in the trees for hours. The air was crisp and seemed to get colder the longer we stayed out in it. The wooden platform was damp and I didn't want to sit on it, so I tried squatting like an Indian or savage or someone I'd seen on TV, but I couldn't do that for too long with my legs aching. My father kept whispering at me to be quiet. They sat in chairs and looked intently over a field. I didn't know what to do, and whatever it was that I was doing was wrong. My father would wave his hand at me to knock it off and I'd have to find something else to occupy my mind with for a few minutes.

The only time I was interested in anything was right before the sun came up, when the sky started to get light but you couldn't see the sun. I thought it was the most amazing thing I'd ever seen. I still do. Light with no visible source of light. I know it's a simple thing, but there's something almost magical about it; it almost gives you hope. So I watched the sky go from black to gray to blue to orange to blue again, and Froehmer and my father saw nothing, at least nothing they were looking for. We sat there for another hundred hours or more and then Froehmer started packing away his guns and we left.

"I was hoping to shoot something," my father said.

"Sometimes it's like that," Froehmer said. "Most times. I like being out in the quiet. I don't need to take a shot." He immediately regretted saying that. "I would have liked you to get one though. We'll go out again. You'll get one." We never went back out.

We stopped at a diner and Froehmer and my father ordered big plates of food, steak and eggs and corned beef hash and toast. I had silver dollar pancakes and a small glass of juice. Froehmer took his cup of coffee and slid it across the table to me. "Give that a try," he said. "He couldn't sit still all morning, now you're going to pump him full of coffee?" "He'll be all right," Froehmer said. I took a sip and put the cup back on the table. Froehmer took it and put milk and sugar in it until it was more milk and sugar than coffee. "You'll like it now," he said and I did.

"I don't remember the hunting part of it," I told my father, "but I remember Froehmer gave me coffee for the first time at breakfast."

"You squirmed so much you chased all the deer away," my father said, teasing me. "I don't know if Froehmer knew what the hell he was doing. I sure didn't. He did his part back then though, didn't he? But I'm the one that gave you the coffee. You don't remember?"

I remembered. I knew who gave it to me. The same way I remembered Froehmer, about four years later, giving me my first beer. I walked in on him and my father talking in the kitchen. They were sitting at the table looking over some paper with a six-pack in front of them. They weren't expecting me, that's for sure, but Froehmer, as natural and smooth as anything handed me a beer and said, "Take this and join us."

As I was sitting down, he slid the paper off the table and put it in his coat pocket. I had no idea what they had been talking about or what they'd been looking at. Looking back, I'm sure they were looking over their pad, who paid them (and how much) and more important, who owed them and how much.

I took the bottle and let it sit in front of me. I didn't look at my father, not wanting to see if he was disappointed or not. I watched Froehmer. I watched how he held the beer casually in his hand, how he grabbed it lightly high up on the neck, with only his thumb and forefinger, and how he tipped it to his lips. I counted the seconds between each time he took a drink. I tried to imitate him, but immediately knew it wouldn't work. I didn't think I could get the bottle from the table to my own lips with only two fingers the way Froehmer had done.

The bottle was heavy and cumbersome in my fingers. So I grabbed it low, my palm and all five fingers pressed firmly around the bottle and hefted it to my mouth. I liked the taste immediately; I liked it even better by the end. I took my first drink and counted to forty-two then took another. Froehmer and my father were talking but I have no idea about what. I was too busy counting to another forty-two. I wanted another one. My father looked at me and then at Froehmer, and then, not looking at either one of us said, "Don't make a habit of it."

"I remember," I told my father.

"You don't remember the half of it, not one iota of it. No one knows what we did. All the good we did. And a little of the bad." He smiled at that. "Froehmer did all right, let me tell you."

"He seems like he's still doing all right," I said.

"And look at me. Look at him and look at me. I gave a lot, you know that? Maybe I gave too much. Look at this crap." He held up his arm with the tubes coming out of it. "It's not what we signed up for, is it, son?"

"It'll be all right, Pop."

"But will it be all right for us? That's the question. Take what you can now, kid, cause you don't know how it will all end up. Take it from Froehmer, even, if you have to. I know he's helped you, but I helped him more, believe me. Whatever he says you owe him; he owes me twice as much, ten times as much. I hope he comes to see me. I'll tell him to his face. I hope he comes."

Maybe that's why Froehmer wouldn't come. I don't know. Who would want to hear any of that? Who'd want to see it? I didn't say anything to Froehmer, and didn't bring him up again with my father. I continued on as before. Froehmer was doing all right by me so far. I wasn't going to be greedy. I'd take the small things handed to me, just like I'd always done.

4

THE ENVELOPE

IN THE EARLY DAYS OF THE OPERATION, I WOULD DO THE WORK AND A FEW DAYS LATER FROEHMER WOULD MEET ME AT THE DINER. After a cup of coffee, or maybe breakfast, he'd get up and walk out and leave an envelope on his seat. He also always left the check, always. I never cared; there was the envelope. We never talked about how much would be in the it; I always left that to him and he was always fair. After a while, it wasn't Froehmer waiting in the diner, but somebody else, somebody who worked for him, like me.

I knew other people worked for Froehmer, but he never talked about them except in vague, indirect ways. "I'll have someone look into that," he might say, or "I think someone can help with that," so I knew I was part of a larger organization, but I didn't really think of myself as part of it, and I didn't care. I didn't care who else was part of it or what they did or if I would ever meet them. I did my work and left it at that. I did what Froehmer said, and that was the extent of it. But now there was someone else, sitting in Froehmer's seat and leaving me with the check for breakfast, and maybe taking something out of the envelope before it got to me. I had to talk about terms and transactions and all those things. Fairness was out of it now. Scores were being kept.

I didn't care as long as the envelopes kept coming. After Frank joined we never saw Froehmer; it was always the same guy sitting in the diner, Mobley. He was five years older than I was and had been working for Froehmer about as long as I had, I guess. I don't really know. I don't know where he came from, or how he got to be with Froehmer. The same way I did, maybe. I didn't really care. I didn't know anything about him, other than he was Froehmer's errand boy. And the fact that he always had an attitude around me, a hostility he figured put me at a disadvantage. He was about the same build, a little taller. I thought I could take him in a fair fight, if it ever came to that. But nothing would be fair with Mobley. You knew that by looking at him. He would do whatever he had to do, or whatever Froehmer told him. Mobley had a face you could put on a penny, calm and composed, but he was not to be fucked with. He had that air about him too, which is why he was sitting there across from us at the diner. "He's a stick of dynamite," Frank had said about him. "He looks harmless enough, but you know he can take your head off." Frank thought it best if I went to the diner by myself. "Why should both of us get blown up?" he half-teased me.

And then Mobley stopped wanting to meet at the diner. He'd pick some parking lot, or driveway, or street corner and I'd have to go out of my way and he'd hand over the envelope and I'd go on my way. It was better. There was never anything to talk with Mobley about anyway, so why have coffee together, why sit across from each other like we knew each other?

"Do you have a problem with me?" I asked Mobley directly one day.

"I don't have a problem," he said.

"So what is it then?"

"I don't like you," he said, very matter-of-fact. And that was that.

IIIII

It was around then that I started to go over and give some money for the kid. I'd count out enough for Frank and me and put a little bit back in the envelope and drive over to Denise's. She was clean again, or so I'd heard, and back on her own, so maybe she could be trusted. I was still going to meetings at that time, so maybe it was part of making amends, or maybe because I was more sympathetic to what she'd gone through, was going through, or maybe I was trying to take more responsibility. Maybe I didn't want the past weighing on me ("You can't change the past; you can only change the present," is one of those clichés they tell you in recovery). Maybe it was all of that. "However you got here, it's good," Frank said. He supported me giving Denise and Eva money, but he never went with me.

Denise would look past me standing on her stoop and look at the car. "Frank still around?"

"Frank's still around."

"I thought maybe Froehmer would have run him off by now."

I let it pass. "Is Eva around?"

"No," Denise said.

"She doing all right?"

"We're okay." She didn't want to talk; she wanted the envelope and that was it.

"I was thinking we could set up an account for Eva, so I wouldn't have to come by all the time. I could just put everything in her account."

"If that's what you want. I thought you wanted to see her once in a while."

"I could still do that," I said. "I thought she'd be here today."

"No. Not today."

"I could come back."

"If you want," she said. "If you're not too busy doing errands for Froehmer."

"It's what I do," I said, not taking her hook.

"As long as you know what you're doing, and who for."

"I know."

"I don't think you do," she said. "Fair warning."

"Okay." I handed her the envelope.

"I'll put it in the bank myself," she said. "I'll show you the statements if you want."

"That's okay."

"The fuck it is," she said and closed the door.

That's how it went most of the time. Sometimes it was better. Sometimes I saw Eva.

5

THE TARGET

FRANK AND I HADN'T WORKED IN ALMOST A WEEK WHEN FROEHMER TOLD ME ABOUT THE JOB OUT OF TOWN.

"I'll get you a hotel and a car." He took out his pencil and wrote the name of the hotel and an address. "It's a small job. But I'll make it worth your while. Double the usual."

"Okay."

"A quick trip. Be back by Friday."

I didn't say anything.

"Shouldn't be a problem," Froehmer said. "It's a small thing. It's easy."

"If it's so easy why do you need me?"

Froehmer patted me on the back. "Let me know when you're ready and I'll give you the details."

"I know."

"Be back no later than Friday."

Maybe he was anxious, I don't know. He seemed anxious. Or I should say that now, remembering it, he seemed anxious. At the time, I didn't notice anything, or ignored it when I should have been paying attention. None of it was usual – going out of town, a tighter schedule than normal, extra money – so why should Froehmer be his usual self? Why should I be? None of it mattered, of course, until it did. None of it should have mattered. Froehmer was right; it was easy. The job was always easy. It was everything else that turned out to be the problem.

IIIII

We had wasted Wednesday, or Frank had, but we were ready; we could still make it back to Froehmer on time. Frank would have to accept the prep I'd done without him, and I wasn't sure he would. He let me know early how well he thought I'd done without him.

We woke up and were over at the address before the sun was up. We sat in the car and watched the house. Frank did a sweep for cameras with a homemade device he'd always used. It always worked.

"You walked around?" he said.

"There's a window near the back door we can use," I said.

"There's a camera over the back door," he said.

I hadn't noticed. That's why I had Frank. If he'd been around the day before, if he'd been paying attention to what he was getting paid to do . . .

"It's not operational," Frank said.

"Now or yesterday?"

"Both," Frank said. That was his way of reminding me that I should have already scanned the place. I knew how to do it; Frank had taught me. But I hadn't done it. It had been a mistake and even if it was inconsequential it was still important.

|||||

Frank finished his scan of the target and I handed him a coffee. We watched the house. Lights came on. The sun came up. Lights went off. My coffee was long gone. I fidgeted like a kid without a gun sitting in a deer stand. Something was wrong with me. I was tired, that was it. I closed my eyes and went to sleep for twenty minutes. Frank would watch. I wouldn't miss anything anyway. I had time. I opened my eyes. Frank was still watching the house.

"What do you want to do?" he said without looking at me.

"When?"

"When we get back home."

"I hadn't thought about it," I said, knowing he had.

"Maybe we could go somewhere."

"You like hotel living."

"I could use a break," Frank said. "You?"

"Sure. Where would we go?"

"I've got a place in mind," Frank said and didn't say anything more.

"Some place with water," I said.

"I know a place."

I could wait. It's what I do. If you think about it, most of your time is spent waiting. Waiting for work to end, waiting for the day to end, waiting for a train, a plane, a taxi, a bus, waiting to get home, waiting for somebody else to get home, waiting to eat, waiting to go to bed, waiting for someone to say what you want to hear. We spend all our time waiting for one thing to stop and waiting for something else to start. Maybe you're waiting for me to get to the point. The point is, as Frank liked to remind me, there is no such thing as waiting. Not really. Not if you do it right. Waiting is nothing more than preparation. And as someone else has said, success is nothing more than opportunity plus preparation. And being prepared means being ready when opportunity arrives. Or leaves, in our case. We watch the house; we know the house; and then wait for everybody to leave. As far as we were concerned, that was the job. What we took wasn't ours anyway. We did that for Froehmer. The rest we did for us. I wasn't tired anymore. I was ready. I sent Froehmer a message and he sent back the details of what he wanted.

|||||

A man and a boy came out of the house. The man had a messenger bag over his shoulder and the boy had a small backpack. Father and son headed off to work and school. The son was a teenager, a high school kid, we figured. Not college, though he looked old enough. The father was a lot older than the boy. He was around Froehmer's age, I'd guess. "Second wife," Frank said and we waited for her to leave. She came out of the house almost a half hour later. At least fifteen years younger than the husband, I thought. I hadn't noticed it the day before. "Second wife," Frank said with absolute confidence.

"My father almost had a second wife," I said.

"I haven't heard this before," Frank said. "When was that?"

"About a year after my mother died. He was lonely. That's what he said. He met this woman, divorced with a couple of kids. He asked her to marry him. My father asked me what I thought about it – I wasn't even nine – and I asked him if he loved her. He said no, that he didn't want to be alone. He didn't want me to be alone. I told him that he shouldn't get married if he didn't love her. He asked her anyway."

"She said no?"

"She said wait. She said it was too soon. So they waited. Then she got tired of waiting, I guess, and moved on. And my father got used to being lonely."

"Your whole life would have been different, you know."

"Maybe. Maybe I'd be respectable."

"Not that different," Frank said. "You've got the blood of a thief in you."

6

THE FATHER

WE'RE ALL BORN THIEVES. Eve and the apple and all that. Jacob and Esau. The Bible has plenty of thieves in it; Christ is even described as arriving like a thief, and he's crucified between two thieves, one of them even gets promised Heaven. I've been in enough hotels to know the Gideon. And I know that if there's something to be stolen, it's been taken at one time or another. Buddha's tooth, St. Catherine's head, Jesus' foreskin, you name it. Museums are filled with the work of thieves, things stolen from ancient civilizations like Greece or Rome or Egypt. The Romans stole from the Egyptians, obelisks and whatever else they wanted. Hell, there's a pyramid in the middle of Rome. Entire countries have been stolen. America stole most of its land, from Indians and Mexicans and whoever else stood in their way ("Property is theft!"). Everybody steals, especially the rich. What was it that Meyer Lansky said? "Look at the Astors and the Vanderbilts, all those big society people. They were the worst thieves." Nobody got rich working.

Businessmen, inventors, and artists steal anything and everything. Filmmakers, painters, writers, most of them wouldn't have created anything without ripping off someone else. Musicians have stolen from each other probably as far back as the muses – Elvis and Led Zeppelin would never have amounted to anything if they hadn't been blatant thieves – and writers take what they need ("immature poets imitate; mature poets steal"). And governments, well, you know they take whatever they want. I always thought it was Dylan who said that if you steal a little they put you in jail, but if you steal a lot they make you a king, but Frank says that it was Eugene O'Neill. Maybe Dylan stole it from Gene and he stole it from someone else. Nothing belongs to anyone; it all just gets passed around from hand to hand, and keeps going long after we're gone. It's the theft of the thing that keeps it going, gives it value and history, and lasts.

We all steal something; it's the way we are. My father was a thief, I guess, but more of a crook. He worked at a desk in City Hall as a building inspector. He took kickbacks and bribes and took what he could out of the budget, a little here and there, enough to raise suspicions but never enough to get caught outright. He was investigated twice, but nothing ever came of it. He was dirty, and didn't mind people knowing, as long as they couldn't prove it. "You can't get greedy," he said. "Take a little but still do your job and nobody cares. It's the guys who take too much that get themselves in trouble."

IIIII

"You don't need much to get by in the world," Frank said one time when we were watching a target. We were sitting in the parking lot of a self-storage facility, a series of huge warehouses where people bought space to store stuff they'd probably never look at ever again. "It's like renting a dump," Frank said. "Most people have too much." "Plenty of people don't have enough," I said. "The world can deal with lack," Frank said. "What we haven't figured out is how to deal with excess."

"My father would have liked you," I said.

"I doubt it."

"You think like him," I said, "but you express it better. College education. He would have liked that."

"He went?"

"Not my father. Trade school. He was smart though. Read a lot, like you. Knew a lot about a lot of stuff, like you. Was always trying to figure everything out, like you, see all the angles. He wanted me to go to college. That was a big disappointment, believe me."

"Junior college. That's not nothing."

"Only one year. Then I quit and went to work, for the baby on the way."

"I still can't believe that."

"Everybody makes mistakes. Mine just happen to be bigger."

"You talked about getting married?"

"Never. I wanted to help out, but she didn't want it. She wanted the money, but she didn't want anything else. Then she met up with the wrong guy. Then the money wasn't going to the kid, so . . ."

We watched the rent-a-dump some more. The big metal buildings were lit up and looked fake, like part of a movie set. It was late, the time when you say stuff maybe you shouldn't. But it was true. My father would have liked Frank, under the right circumstances. He would have liked him better than me, I think. They had more in common. Frank had done a lot of the same things my father had, a lot of the things my father wished I'd done. I should have kept quiet, but I kept talking. "There was a guy in town when I was growing up who got caught stealing money out of the parking meters," I told Frank. "He had figured out how to skim money out of the machines somehow, and stole thousands. Tens of thousands. All in dimes and quarters. He thought he had it figured out, but somebody noticed and went looking for the missing money. The guy had figured out to steal money all right, but then he went and took too much. Something like sixty thousand. All in change. My father said you had to admire the guy, a little, hauling all those dimes and quarters around. But the guy got greedy, so he got himself arrested and went to prison. 'Take enough,' my father said, 'but never take more than that.' That's something you'd say," I told Frank.

"I wish I'd met him," Frank said.

IIIII

I don't know when my father became a thief. Maybe he started young like me, or maybe he didn't start stealing until after my mother died, or maybe he started stealing for her. I remember him joking about things he'd bring home, a gift for my mother, a nice bottle of wine for dinner, something a little extra, and he'd say, "compliments of Uncle Sam." I didn't think anything about it when I was young. My father worked for the government, so everything was sort of "compliments of Uncle Sam." And I didn't suspect until I was in high school and began to think I knew how things worked.

Personally, I don't think my father began to steal until after my mother died. People steal for all sorts of reasons, desperation, opportunity, revenge, jealousy. I think my father stole because of resentment. He's one of those guys who starts work at some place just fine, no problems, no temptations, but the longer he works the more he sees how many people aren't pulling their weight, and who are making more money, but he continues to work hard and work clean; then he sees the waste and inefficiency and incompetence and that he can't get ahead. Everyone else seems to be doing better, working less. So he starts to take a little extra. There's a system in place for that, especially in government, a way to take something here and there and it won't get noticed. It's the way it's always been and everybody else is getting theirs anyway.

IIIII

My mother died when she was thirty. A drunk hit her out on the highway. I remember sitting with my father at the visitation, the weird funeral home room stuffed with people and everyone silent, the closed casket sitting there in front of all of us, and my father looking at the casket with an odd expression on his face, a quizzical look, like a man trying to read a sign in a foreign language. "That's all it takes," he said and he snapped his fingers with a sound like a whip cracking in the dry air.

He boxed up all of my mother's things only a few days after the funeral, all of her clothes, pictures, toiletries, even her toothbrush, everything went into boxes and we carried them down to the basement. "You can always throw something out," my father said, "but you can't get it back." Every single box is still in the basement, unopened. Now I have to deal with them. Now I have to pack up all his things.

My father died a young man, diseased out before he was fifty. I sat in the hospital with him watching him waste away, thinking I wouldn't be like him. I thought I would be better than him, have a better life.

"It wasn't so long ago that there'd be a line of people wanting to see me," my father said, sitting in his hospital room. All the men who came and went from the house, all the people that waited to see him in his office, none of them came now. No one came to the hospital but me. "People do what they can," I said.

"People do what they can get away with," my father said. "Like you. When's the last time you saw your kid?"

It had been a while. "I'll get over there as soon as you're out of here," I said.

"I left a little for the kid," he said. "In the will."

He was watching TV when he said it, not looking at me. He turned the sound up before he spoke again.

"There's not much," he said. "Not as much as there should be, I'll tell you that. So don't get any ideas. You're going to have to work, you know what I mean?"

"You haven't figure out how to take it with you?"

"I could use a little of it too," he said, "just to get through the gates, maybe." He laughed at that.

He always had envelopes of cash laying around, under the bed, under the couch, under the silverware tray in the kitchen drawer, under the car seat. A couple hundred bucks in each white envelope. All my life, I never took a single bill. I think it disappointed my father. So, when he was lying there in his casket and a parade of men passed in front of him, I saw one of the guys slip a white envelope into his suit jacket, a gesture of respect, a little token for the afterlife, maybe. When everyone had gone I went up and lifted the envelope and took a few bills off the top – I wasn't going to take all of it – and put the rest back in the envelope and put it in his suit. I had to leave something for him to take with him, an obol for the ferryman Charon, something to get him through the gates. I took just enough to make him happy, I thought, out of respect. To show him that I'd learned a thing or two. To let him know he didn't have to worry.

That parade of men – contractors, masons, electricians, plumbers, carpenters, roofers, shop owners, city employees, all the men he had worked with over the years – many of them were the ones who used to come and go at the house. They all came to the visitation; they all came to the funeral. Not one of them came to the hospital. Except Froehmer. He didn't come to any of it.

I don't know if my father had any friends. He wasn't the friendly type. He didn't socialize; he didn't have hobbies. He'd go fishing or hunting if someone asked (usually Froehmer) but he'd never initiate it. He must have gone out, but I don't remember it. I never remember him saying "my friend" when talking about anyone. It was always what they did, or where they were from. "Ustico, the plumber," or "Sweeney from the Board of Ed." It was about what they did. The men who came and went in and out of the house, the men who paraded past his dead body, they were business associates, colleagues, acquaintances. I don't know if he ever thought of one of them as anything more than someone he worked with, someone he did something for, someone who owed him money. I don't think a single one of them was a friend. A friend is there when you need them; a friend visits you in the hospital. A friend carries your casket at your funeral. Or at least makes an appearance. Froehmer sent flowers. And an envelope.

Froehmer had always been there, as long as I could remember. He'd been there for my father and he'd been there for me. I couldn't figure it out. I still haven't.

"You never know how someone will react to death," Frank told me. "People don't act like themselves sometimes."

"You think I should give him a pass?"

"That's not what I mean," Frank said. "You should place it in context of how he's acted all the time you've known him."

I tried to think of it that way. Froehmer would do more for me, more than even my own father.

|||||

My father was right about his money. There wasn't as much as I thought. A lot of it had gone to medical, I knew that, some of it had gone to the funeral arrangements. Maybe he'd spent the rest, maybe he never had as much as he wanted everyone to believe. Maybe he figured out how to take it with him after all. There should have been more, it seemed to me, but there wasn't. I emptied out his bank account, then I went around the house and found as many of his envelopes as I could. Then I left town. I wasn't going to look back, and I didn't. What I left behind caught up with me anyway.

After about a year, I was in a nice amount of debt and had a small drug habit. I had to sell my father's house for about half what I should have gotten and was scrounging around trying to scrape enough together from one day to the next just to keep the habit going. I had no permanent place to stay, no work, no prospects, and no worries. It hadn't started that way – I had thought I would have a better life with a new start away from where I'd been all my life – but it ended with me worse off than before, and not realizing it. I didn't give a shit. I thought I could stop any time, that I didn't want to stop. Change would happen whenever I chose, I thought, but nothing was going to change. Then Froehmer called.

"I'm coming to get you," he said. He drove down and found me and immediately took me to a treatment center.

"I can't do this," I said.

"Not by yourself," he said.

"I mean, I can't afford this."

"You're taken care of."

There was a time when I thought Froehmer did it for my father; there are still times when I think he did it for me; and there are other times when I know he did it for himself. He had a reliable machine that had broken and needed to be fixed – like a trusty old tractor – that's how he thought about it. And the repairs weren't cheap. Froehmer might have done it for me, but not without strings. I was a name in the pad with a debt in the next column.

7
THE FIRE

"HOW'S THE GIRL?" Froehmer asked out of the blue.

We were finishing up breakfast at the diner, and he caught me off guard. It had been a long while since he'd asked about that. It had been years since I had reconnected with Froehmer, four or five years since he had helped me run off trouble when I couldn't, and it had been a long time since he had reminded me of what he'd done for me. I thought we were square. I was hoping he was done with it.

"I don't know," I said. "I haven't seen her."

"You should make the effort," he said.

"That's long done."

Froehmer took the last of his coffee and shook his head with disapproval. "A man should have a good relationship with his children," he said. "You should see the girl."

I thought he was talking about Denise, not Eva. I nodded. "I'll make the effort."

"Think about you and your father," Froehmer said. "It could be like that, or it could be like we were, you know?"

I nodded.

"You liked me coming around, right?"

"Sure," I said.

"Then we lost touch, but we picked right back up. You knew we could reconnect, right? You knew you could reach out when you needed. That's how it could be with the girl. But you have to build that foundation first. It will be better for her. She'll know she can count on you, you know?"

"I'll make the effort."

Froehmer stood up and put his hand on my shoulder for a second, then left. He was right, but it was more complicated than that. Everything always was.

I stood in the hallway of a shitty apartment building and thought about leaving. I could text Denise and tell her that something came up. She wouldn't care. And Eva wouldn't care. I'd seen the kid, I'd made the effort, I'd done the right thing, but this was different. Denise wanted me to take Eva for a couple of hours, just the two of us. I stood in the hallway and thought about bailing. But I didn't. I knocked on the door and they were ready.

"I was starting to wonder," Denise said.

"I'm not that late," I said.

"You're late enough," she said. "I've got things I need to do."

"Okay."

She gave Eva a hug and handed her off to me. “What are you going to do?”

“I thought maybe we’d go to the park,” I said.

“She likes the park. Don’t you, sweets?”

Eva nodded and I took her by the hand and headed back to the car. She looked more like me than the last time I’d seen her. “You can’t outrun your blood,” my father liked to remind me. I took no pride in that. I only hoped that there would be a course correction somewhere, the sooner the better for her. I wouldn’t wish another version of myself on the world. I couldn’t do anything about appearance, but maybe I could help in other ways. That’s why I was there, wasn’t it?

“How’s school?” I asked her.

She was in kindergarten, I think. Maybe not yet. I tried to lead her into the answer, but she wasn’t having any of it. She looked out the passenger window and gave one-word, disinterested responses. I was just a ride to the park. That was fine with me, for now. I wasn’t expecting much; I didn’t want much, just a foundation, like Froehmer had said. The park was about a half mile from the apartment building. We never made it.

The street was blocked off by cops and fire trucks. A house was on fire. You could see the flames coming out of the side of the house, and black smoke pumping out of an open upstairs window. The firemen had just arrived and they worked with quick, steady deliberation to get the hoses set up, the house prepped and cleared, ready to stop the flames and smoke. I started to back up the car and retreat the way we came, but Eva wanted to stay. “I want to watch the firemen,” she said without looking at me. She was already glued to the scene. I pulled over to the curb and put the car in park.

Eva started a steady stream of questions. “What are they doing? Why are they doing that? What are they doing now? Why are they doing that. Why did they go in the house? Why aren’t they turning on the water?” I tried to answer the best I could. I figured if it led to another question, I'd done all right. But maybe Eva didn't care about the answers, only the questions. That wasn't true.

"How did the fire start?" she said.

"I don't know. The firemen will find out."

"Maybe someone started it," Eva said.

"Maybe, but probably not. It was probably an accident."

"Like what?"

"Like someone left the stove on, or left a candle lit. I don't know. Fires can start all sorts of ways."

"They can?"

"Sure," I said and thought better of it. "But almost always it's because someone was careless, or did something they shouldn't."

"Why isn't anyone coming out?"

"I don't think anyone was home."

"Will the firemen take things?"

"What do you mean?"

"The firemen take things from the house."

"They'll just put out the fire."

"They steal things," Eva said. "I saw it on TV. They take things after they put out the fire."

"I don't know about that."

"I saw them," Eva said. "I saw them take things. Watch. You'll see."

So we sat and watched the firemen until the fire was out and the hoses were coiled and put back on the trucks and all the gear was stowed and the men back on the trucks. Everything was ruined in the house, ruined by smoke and water. There would be nothing to take anyway. Maybe some small things, jewelry, silver, coins. I thought about it. Thought how their coats could be stuffed with whatever they found. The trucks left. The house was scarred, a black open wound on one side. Eva didn't say anything. We went to the park, but Eva didn't want to get out of the car.

"Would you go into a house that was on fire?" she said.

"I wouldn't," I said. "Only if I was a fireman. But I'm not."

"What if I was inside?"

"Well, then I'd go in. I'd go in and get you."

"You wouldn't take things, would you? Would you take things from me?"

"I wouldn't even think about it. I'd get you and we'd get away from the fire as fast as we could. That's what you have to do."

"And you wouldn't call the firemen?"

"We'd have to call them," I said. "They'd have to put out the fire."

"I suppose," she said and thought about it some more.

"They're not like the ones you saw before," I said. "They're like the ones we saw today. They didn't take anything, did they?"

"I guess not."

"Besides, your house isn't going to be on fire. You're going to be careful."

"Mom's not careful, though. And her friends. They're not careful."

"They will be," I said. "Tell them to be careful."

"Okay," Eva said.

It was time for her to go back to her mother. On the drive back I thought how it was almost as if I had taken Eva to work with me. We sat in a car and watched a house. She was the one who thought about robbing it. That's what you get for making an effort. She was quiet on the ride back and barely said goodbye to me when we got to the apartment door. She hugged her mother and went into another room. I wasn't invited inside.

"She's tired," Denise said. "I can tell. You must have walked her all over the park."

"We never made it," I said. "She wanted to watch some firemen working."

"She must have loved that."

"She did. She had a lot of questions."

"She has a lot of questions."

"She wanted to know if the firemen were going to rob the place. She told me she saw it on TV."

Denise laughed. "She did see it on TV," she said. "The other night on *The Simpsons*."

I laughed. "She had me thinking it was real."

"She had you thinking," Denise said.

"Not like that. No judgment"

"Yeah, I know how that's a one-way street for you."

I shouldn't have told her. Now we were at a place where we couldn't say anything. I thought I'd done all right, but Denise wasn't so happy about it now, all of a sudden. Fuck it, I thought. I don't need to see her.

"Okay then," I said and left, and spent the rest of the time thinking about Eva and how I wanted to see her.

|||||

I'd met Denise in a waste-of-time class at the community college. I'd wanted to go to trade school, learn something useful like how to be an electrician, but my father wanted me to get an education. "Take a few business classes, learn how the system works," he said. He could have taught me that. He could have taught me better than any of the underpaid, underenthused, uninteresting, uninspiring teachers who droned on in the bland rooms of the community college. "Take a year or two," my father said. "Then, if it's not for you, if you don't want to go on to a university, you can go learn a trade. Then you'll know how to run a business, because I'm telling you, you're not going to be happy working for somebody else. You'll want to run your own shop. If you go that route. But give the classes a shot." He was paying for it, so what could I say? I had to sit in class and try to pay attention.

We weren't in our second week, when she leaned over and said to me, "Am I stupid, or is this class awful?"

"This guy's brilliant," I said. "That's why he's teaching here instead running some Fortune 500 company. He's a genius, we're the morons."

We talked like that for a couple of weeks. She'd say something during class and I'd try to think of something funny to say back. She was nice enough. I didn't know anything more about her than she thought the class was as bad as I did. I didn't think about her, to be honest, and then one day she said, "I'm having a party on Saturday, if you want to come."

"Sure," I said.

"You have to be there by eight," she said. "That's the only thing."

"Okay," I said.

So I showed up at her apartment at eight o'clock on Saturday and there was no one else there. Only her and me.

"How many people do you need to have a party?" she said. She poured some wine and said, "I didn't know what you'd say if I asked you for a date, so I thought I'd see if you'd come over for a party. It's totally casual; you can leave if you want."

I didn't leave, obviously. I had my out and I didn't take it. Instead, I sat where she told me to sit and drank the wine she poured for me and answered all the questions she asked me. I told her that my father worked down at City Hall, that's all I said.

"Oh yeah," she said. "The mayor."

"That's right," I said. "I'm the mayor's son. I always forget."

I knew she was going to ask about my mother next, so I told her before she asked.

"My mother ruins every party," I said but she didn't laugh.

"My parents got divorced when I was about the same age," she said, "and I'm still not used to it."

"Maybe because both parents are still around," I said. "My mom's here, but my father's long gone," she said. "California or Korea, who knows."

IIIII

"College is worse than high school, don't you think?" she said.

"Can I ask you something," I said, "something that's going to sound ruder than I mean."

"Okay," she said, not sure.

"Are you this negative about everything, or just community college?"

She laughed. "It's all I talk about, right? I don't know you well enough to talk about anything else yet, I guess. I'm not a negative person, I don't think. I'm just down on the college classes I took."

"What would you rather do?"

She didn't know. "I've got time to figure it out, don't I. How about you?"

"I wanted to go learn a trade," I said, "Be an electrician, start my own business. I figured my father could help me get started, get some work and get established. I wish he'd just give me the money he's spending for classes and let me do what I want."

"Who's your father?"

I told her and she nodded.

The next time I saw her, she said, "I talked about you and your dad with my mother."

"What did she say about it?" I said.

"She says your dad's a crook."

"White-collar crook," I said. She laughed at that.

"I told her he must not be much of a crook if he won't give you some of that corruption instead of making you go to school."

"He wants me to live a straight life," I said.

"Where's the fun in that?" she said.

That's the way we actually talked, more or less. We talked that way for a couple of months and then we hardly talked at all. She was pregnant and didn't want to talk about it. She left school and didn't want to talk about it. I had to call her months later and ask about the baby. I had to ask her name.

"Eva," she said and that's about it.

"I want to help," I told her. She didn't want my help. I left school and worked on construction sites, a job I'd gotten with the help of my father, and tried to make some money for her. I didn't want to talk about it.

There were always drugs handy on the construction crews; some guys couldn't get through the day without a little something to keep them going, then they couldn't get through the night without something to counteract what they took during the day. Pills got bought and sold, or sometimes handed out like candy. One of the guys called them the "giddyups" and the "giddydowns." I never needed the former, but I did like the latter. I remember the first time they hit me, sitting at a bar with a few of the guys from work, and a few women who someone had invited to join us, and how it was like a switch had been turned on, like a puzzle had been solved. It was an answer I'd been looking for; I could be someone else for a while, not be myself for a change. Whoever I was, whatever else I was feeling or thinking, all the fuck-ups and doubts and hesitations, all of that was off somewhere else, a small shadow in the distance. I could be somebody else as long as I took a pill or two. It was that easy.

I hadn't done any drugs, not much of anything really, except for when I was with Denise, before she was pregnant, I mean. We'd get together, drink some wine, drop a few pills and everything would be all right. What was there to talk about then, when everything is moving nice and everything else is far off and forgotten? Drugs don't fix anything, they only make it seem like everything's been fixed. Sometimes that's enough. Sometimes it's more than enough.

We got fucked up four times and four times we wound up in bed. She kept a box of condoms in the drawer of her bedside table. I knew they weren't one hundred percent, but at first I wasn't sure the kid was mine. She didn't buy that box just for me.

“You’re the only one,” she said.

I found out later that it wasn’t true, but it didn’t change the math on anything.

“Are you ready for this?” I said.

“I’m ready,” she said. “You don’t have to go through with it.”

“I can’t get an abortion,” she said. “I’m Catholic.”

Not Catholic enough, I thought, to do without until you’re married.

“I’m not expecting anything,” she said. “I don’t want to get married, if that’s what you’re worried about. I’m not ready for that.”

We weren’t in love; we weren’t even all that close. We hung out and spent a few nights together and then she got pregnant because nothing is one hundred percent effective.

Frank said, “But you knew that going in. You weren’t really prepared then, not if you didn’t have all the percentages covered.”

My percentages were covered; I could just walk away and leave it all up to her. Denise and I were done. It had all been a big mistake, but it wasn’t about her. It was about the kid. I thought I should do something. Denise tried to let me off the hook. I wouldn’t let myself off, not at first anyway.

“I don’t have to be anything but the kid’s father,” I said, “but at least let me be that.”

I brought her the money every payday and spent time with the baby, but that didn’t last long, and then she met this other guy. I never met him; she never talked about him. I just knew I was out.

“I don’t want you coming around,” she told me.

I knew she was using. The other guy had introduced her to the harder stuff. She liked to tell me that it was none of my business. We had a few fights and she called the cops. It was bad enough that she got a restraining order. She made it a bigger thing than what it was. But I’m not blaming her.

I know I’m responsible for most of the bad in her life. I’m sure that if she could do it all over again she never would have leaned over and talked to me in class. You never know how things are going to turn out. I feel bad for her. But I will also say this: I wanted to be part of her life, to be there for her and the baby. She didn't want it; she thought she could do better than me. She could have. Easy. But she didn't. And that was a problem that got put on me and kept me away from them because of a judge and all that. That's when I called Froehmer. And I was done with her for a while, but it all led me back to her, back to Eva, trying to make up for something, trying to cover some percentages.

8
THE GOAT

I DON'T CARE HOW MUCH PREPARATION YOU DO, YOU CAN NEVER ANTICIPATE THE UNEXPECTED. "I'm not saying you eliminate it, but you minimize its impact," Frank argued. And I might give him shit about his prep, his cautions, his superstitions, but Frank's real talents come into play on the rare occasions when things don't go as planned. The job is easy, I always say; it's everything else that's hard. The job was easy, if you define the job only as taking what we came for. If you define the job as delivering the thing to the man who hired you, well, that's the story here. That's where things got hard.

"We should wait another day," Frank said.

I wanted to tell him that he should have been here yesterday. Instead, I told him that everything was going to be fine. "Tomorrow's a different day. We don't know anything about tomorrow. We only know about today. Everyone's gone. The house is empty. I'll be in and out in five minutes. Tops."

Frank wasn't convinced. He trusted me; he knew I was right, but he hadn't done the preparation himself, so he wasn't one hundred percent certain. He hadn't worked it all out the way he usually did. He hadn't looked at every gear and figured out how the whole machine worked. We'd been in this situation before. Frank and his superstitions. He only needed a little more time. We sat in the car and waited.

The house was there, empty. We watched for a while more. We watched neighbors leave; the whole block seemed to empty out, with kids off to school and parents off to work. We probably could have walked off with everything. We should have brought a truck, I thought. But that's not the way we worked. We didn't want any of their stuff. We only wanted one thing, and I knew what it was and where to find it. Frank did another scan of the house, just to see if anything had changed. Nothing had. He would do this a few more times, right up until I went inside. We watched the man and boy leave the house, and then the woman. If Frank had been here yesterday, I would have followed her. If we'd had more time we would have followed the boy and the man as well. We would know where the man worked, the woman too, and even found out where the boy went to school. We would have called the offices right before I went inside. Just to make sure they were where they were supposed to be. Just so Frank could be sure.

IIIII

It was almost noon by the time Frank was ready. We hadn't even checked out of the hotel. Frank called and wanted to know if we could get a late checkout. After a brief argument he booked another night. “We should go back today,” I told him. “Right when I get back to the car.”

“Let’s stay,” Frank said. “They’re going to charge us for the room anyway,” he said, “whether we’re there or not.”

That was our first mistake. We should have been out of the hotel hours ago. We didn’t even think of it until we were sitting there for hours in the car. There was no reason that we took so much time. Well, there was, but I don’t blame Frank. I go back to me making him move off the horse. That put everything in motion, that was the gear in the machine that made it all click, and that’s on me. You see how one decision can affect everything that comes after.

“We’ll get back in time,” Frank said, still trying to convince me. “When did Froehmer say?”

“Before noon,” I told him. Froehmer hadn’t said what time.

“He can wait for once,” Frank said, then, “We’ll be back. We’ll be back with time to spare. Froehmer will get his. The way he always does.”

I decided I couldn’t wait any more. “I’m going in,” I said, “if that’s all right with you.”

“I don’t know why you’re not back already,” Frank said.

There was no one on the street, no neighbors looking out the windows. I got out of the car and walked directly to the back of the house, directly to the window I noticed the day before. I saw the small camera on the back stoop, above the door. It was old, probably hadn’t been used in years. There was the decal of a home security company in the window of the back door, a blue shield with white initials. They let it all lapse once they got comfortable. Probably a safe neighborhood.

I pried the screen out of the window jamb and sure enough, the window was unlocked, just the way I’d found it the day before, and I slid it open and crawled through into the kitchen. I moved straight through the kitchen, walked through the dining room and took a look in the living room. I walked down the hallway and there was a small office. There was a desk, a small couch against one wall, and some bookcases. The shelves of the bookcases had a few family photographs and other crap. I scanned the shelves and there was what we'd been sent for, sitting right there in front of me. I knew it was going to be easy.

It was a small statue of a goat, a cheap silver animal trophy that had roman numerals engraved on it and a bunch of initials, an abbreviation for something. I didn't really pay that much attention to it, to be honest; I didn't really care. It's what we came for, so I took it and put it in my shoulder bag and walked back through the house and crawled back out the window. I replaced the screen and walked down the sidewalk and around the corner, where Frank was waiting.

I handed him the bag so he could look for himself. "Nothing worth much here," I said. "Nothing valuable anyway."

"It's the things that don't have any value that are worth the most," Frank said like he was a sage sitting on the top of some fucking mountain. "Something I read in a fortune cookie," he joked, but it was something he'd said before, something he believed.

"You worried about it?"

"Not yet," Frank said, "but I'm working on it."

We started back to the hotel and Frank began brooding. We wouldn't be able to get back fast enough. We almost didn't get back at all.

|||||

"Stuff that has value can be replaced," he had said. "A house, car, money. Almost anything you can buy, you can buy again. But sentimental stuff, family stuff, ex-girlfriend stuff, your kid's first drawing, whatever means something that no one would care about but you, that's the stuff that's worth the most. Think about it. If you could only take one thing in the world with you, what would it be?"

Frank was not sentimental about those types of things, material objects. Over the years I had become less sentimental, I suppose, but I think I know what Frank would want to save. If he could take one thing, maybe it would be a book. Plato's *Republic*, maybe. But that's not right. He could replace a book; no, he would take something that wasn't his. He'd take my jacket. He'd given it to me anyway. A vintage black leather jacket I wore almost year round. That's the thing he would take. So he could give it back to me, probably.

He already knew my answer. It was a money clip I kept in my pocket. My father had given it to me. His father had given it to him. It had initials engraved on it. It was scratched and bent and wasn't worth any more than the stainless steel that went into making it, but it was maybe the most important thing I owned. My father gave it to me the day I cashed my first paycheck, and I've never gone a day since without it being in my pocket.

"What would you do if someone took that from you?" Frank said.

"Whatever it took to get it back. But this isn't that. You think?"

IIIII

Frank opened the shoulder bag and looked at the small silver goat statue and put it on the seat between us. "Well, it's worth enough for someone wanting it stolen. And that means someone knows more about it than we do." Frank never liked to be in that position. "This isn't good," he said. "This is trouble."

"We'll give it to Froehmer and then it will be his trouble." I put the statue back in the bag and put it in the backseat. "This isn't any trouble at all. Not for us."

Frank nodded but he wasn't convinced. And the trouble came that proved me wrong.

IIIII

We were about four blocks from the house, halfway through an intersection when I saw the car out of the corner of my left eye, coming through the stop sign, speeding right for us. Frank saw it too and I felt him hit the gas, but it was too late. The car collided with us, hitting us squarely at the rear tire, pushing us in an arc through the street that was over in a matter of seconds.

"You all right?" Frank said, after we came to a full stop.

"I'm all right."

"Stay here," Frank said and got out of the car. He walked toward the car that had hit us. I looked over my shoulder but couldn't see much except the airbag in the other car and Frank standing by the driver's door. He wasn't gone for more than a few seconds and came back and leaned in and told me what to do.

"Take our stuff and I'll meet you back at the hotel," he said. He looked up and down the street. There weren't any gawkers, yet. "Go on," he said. "I've got this."

I grabbed our two bags and walked away, not really knowing where to go or how exactly to get back to the hotel. I wasn't thinking. I wasn't thinking about the right things, and before I knew it I had turned down the street where we'd just come from, down the street where the house was. I turned back and kept walking. I could hear the sirens approaching. Frank would deal with all that. I just had to get back to the hotel.

I walked for a good twenty minutes before I saw a cab. By the time I got back to the room, Frank had texted me. "The rental has a broken back wheel/axle. Waiting for a tow. Everything else is good."

Out of habit, I put the bag with the trophy in the safe. I packed our stuff and put it in the closet and closed the door. I sent Froehmer a message. "In hand. Trouble with the car. Will update asap." I saw that he'd read it and the message disappeared. I sat in a chair and held my phone in my hands and waited. I waited an hour. Then I waited another hour. I tried to be like Frank and think through it all, from the moment I got back into the car, to the crash, to me getting back to the hotel. I tried to think about what I knew and forget about the things I didn't know. I tried not to think about the cops, the driver, all the things that could have gone more wrong. Frank never wanted us to use a rental; he didn't understand why Froehmer had insisted on it, even if it was with someone else's name. The whole thing had been done as other people, the hotel, the car, the driver's license. Frank always insisted. "You know how they caught Timothy McVeigh?" he had lectured me. "He had an expired registration tag on his getaway car. One overlooked detail and the whole thing fell apart." There was nothing to worry about, I told myself. The worst we'd done was steal a little trophy; we hadn't blown up a federal building. Besides, Frank wasn't as dumb as Timothy McVeigh. Still, I tried not to think of Frank in trouble and me unable to help. There was no trouble, I kept telling myself.

Frank finally texted. "No cars available. Nothing. Done waiting. See you soon."

I couldn't stay in the room any longer and went out and stood on the street near the front of the hotel and watched the people pass and looked at every approaching cab. It was late afternoon. I texted Froehmer. "Everything good. Rental broke down. No car til tomorrow." Froehmer replied. "No worries. See you then." There was nothing to worry about now. We'd leave the next day and hand the thing over to Froehmer and get paid and wait for the next job. We had a minor hiccup, that was all. A guy ran an intersection. We weren't hurt. It didn't mean anything. I'd have to make sure Frank knew it didn't mean anything. We could do a lot more jobs like this, I thought; we could come into the city, get what Froehmer wanted and get back home. We could do this all day long. It was easy money. That's what I thought. I think too much, or not enough, or just enough to get it all wrong.

I never saw Frank get out of the cab. He was just there, on the sidewalk next to me. "Everything all right?" he said.

"I'm good," I said. "You okay?"

He shrugged. "We got what we came for. We could leave, rent a car from someone else, take a bus. We could go home."

"Let's stay," I said. The room was paid for, Froehmer was taken care of, and I didn't really want to get back in a car. I was still shaken. It wasn't bothering Frank. The guy who'd lost a day worried about a dead horse wasn't worried now at all. For him the job was done.

"Let's go get something to eat," Frank said.

We walked around until we found something that looked all right. "If Froehmer's got a problem," Frank said. "Tell him it was my fault."

"A guy hit us. That's not your fault. I never saw the driver, who was it?"

"Teenager," Frank said. "On the phone."

"Cops?"

"They were more interested in him than me."

"The driver didn't say anything about me?"

"Nothing. Probably never saw you. He wasn't real sure what had happened, but he told the cops right away that he was on the phone. Once he said that I could have driven off in the squad car for all the attention they gave me."

"Lucky for us, I guess," I said.

"I saw him, though," Frank said.

"I know. I felt you hit the gas."

"I didn't see him soon enough." That bothered him. "That's my fault," Frank said.

"Fifty-fifty, like always."

Frank took a look at his watch. "We could still leave tonight," he said.

"It's fine," I said. "We'll go first thing tomorrow."

When we got back to the hotel room Frank read a book he'd brought along. I stared into my phone at some game before I picked up one of Frank's books. I don't remember what it was or what it was about. I was thinking about something my father had told me when he was in the hospital.

"In the end," he said, "People don't really care about how it turned out for you. I mean, some people might be happy, and some other people might be mad, or jealous, or whatever. But in the end, they don't really care one way or the other. They only care about themselves. So if they don't care, if it doesn't really matter, why play by the rules? If they don't care, why should we?"

I don't know why I thought of it. At another time I would have talked to Frank about it. It was exactly the kind of conversation he liked. I didn't say anything. Frank was off somewhere else, lost in his reading. I couldn't concentrate. My head was stuck on something, a shadow of something my father had told me. I thought that maybe I was the only one who cared, and I didn't want to believe it. I wanted to change my own mind for once, to work it out on my own. I fell asleep before anything had changed.

9
THE CAR

WHEN WE'RE ON A JOB, I BET NINETY PERCENT OF OUR TIME IS SPENT IN THE CAR. We might spend more time in the car than we do anywhere else, including our apartment. I had a truck my father bought me when I first started, then a van when I was hauling stuff off work sites, but a van's no good for what we do now. It draws too much attention sitting around for hours. Besides, I lost everything anyway before I got cleaned up and started over again. I knew we needed something that no one would notice. The last thing Frank and I wanted to spend money on was a car, but we sucked it up and went out and bought a car no one pays any attention to, a car you see everywhere, a nondescript Honda Civic. Frank tinted the windows so we could sit and not be noticed or bothered. We sit and watch and sit and watch for hours and hours, entire days might go by in the car. We eat and sleep in the car when we have to. But mostly we sit and watch, in silence. Frank knows when to keep quiet and when to talk, to break the monotony, to jumpstart the brain, to talk about things we need to talk about.

"I can't do this forever," Frank said. It was a conversation we had when Frank was particularly bored, tired of sitting in a car for a couple of days, tired of waiting for Froehmer or someone else to call, tired of whatever routine we had, the way everyone gets tired of their day-to-day. "I can't do this," he said. "Not long-term."

"No one's asking you."

"You have plans for us?"

We all know I'm not the planning type. "What would you rather be doing?"

"Go back to teaching, maybe. Go back to Italy. We could live in Italy. We could live anywhere. I don't know. If I had it figured out, I'd be doing it instead of talking about it. But I know we need to have a plan. This is going to get played out some day, one way or another."

He was right, of course, but Frank had options. He could go back to teaching; he could go and do a lot of things. What could I do? I didn't have any experience with anything else. And I didn't have skills, not for a real job. If I could I'd go back and start all over. I'd stay in school, and not fuck up. I couldn't say that to Frank. They don't like to hear that shit in treatment; you're supposed to look ahead. Tomorrow's going to be better than today, that's the kind of crap they want you to think. Believe me, I'm not convinced that tomorrow is guaranteed to be better, but I know the past could have been. I know I carry it around with me all the time. What I did then has got me where I am now. And I'm not complaining – my life is better than it ever was – but I also know that I'm making the best with what I have. My options are limited, at best.

"What would you do, if you weren't doing this?" Frank said.

"Probably sit around like I usually do," I told him. I couldn't do it forever, but I could sit around and do nothing, especially if it were someplace warm, near some water. "Italy was good, wasn't it? I wasn't the one who had trouble in Italy, as I recall," I said.

"It wasn't the same, not at all," Frank said. "You know that. We should go back. I'll show you."

"Whatever we do," I said, "let's do it outside a fucking Civic."

"No Civics in Italy," Frank said. "Not like here, anyway."

10
THE WATCH

WE'D GONE TO ITALY A COUPLE OF YEARS AGO. We spent a week on the Amalfi coast. It was a place John Steinbeck said would be ruined if visited by more than five hundred people at a time. There were probably twenty times that. The narrow roads cut into the side of the rock cliffs were tire to tire with tour buses, cars, motorcycles, scooters, bicycles, anything with wheels, all moving in impatient jerks and jolts. The sidewalks were not much better, crowded with pedestrians walking in all directions, or worse, standing and taking selfie after selfie and holding up everyone else. It was crowded and chaotic and it was not ruined. There was nothing, it seemed, that could undermine the inherent calm of the place, quiet buildings dug into the steep hills – some of them have been there hundreds of years, outlasting this army and that – the boats that floated in the bay the way they had for centuries, the blue calm of the eternal sea that seemed to wash up to the shore and into the air and over the top of the cliffs continuing on into the calm blue sky. You couldn't ruin any of that, but they sure did try.

We stayed above the chaos and crowds, in a hotel named after Neptune, overlooking the bright houses, the majolica-domed church, the slender strip of sand and the Tyrrhenian Sea. We would have breakfast at the hotel in the morning and then walk down the two hundred or so steps to the beach, sit under the sun or under an orange and blue umbrella until it was time for lunch. We would make our way back to the hotel, shower and walk to some place to eat. Then go back to the hotel and sit by the pool until it was time for a nap or we needed to escape the heat. Frank preferred the pool; I liked the beach. I wanted to watch the waves. I was as white as paper; I would have burned myself to ash if it hadn't been for Frank. It's an overly precious way of saying it, I realize, but I like the phrase. He would set up the umbrella, remind me to "apply sunscreen regularly," and slightly fuss over me in ways that were newly endearing. The waves came and went in their steady procession. I watched them with great satisfaction. I get poetic thoughts in my head, the bright sun on the waves, repeating over and over makes me think how easy it would be to be free, free of our life, free from Froehmer and the men like him who pick up the phone and get all they want and think it's easy because of people like us. I don't begrudge Froehmer anything. I don't regret how we live, Frank and me. I only think about how easy it would be to leave it behind.

It's easy to think that way when you're relaxing on the Italian sand in a nice hotel where they kept you satisfied and Frank's there fussing over me and almost everything is right with the world. Except it's not easy. Frank and I live from job to job, making more money than most, and more than the effort we put into it, but less than you might think. We scrape by in a one-bedroom apartment and watch what we spend. Italy was the first trip in all the time we've worked together. Frank thought about putting it all on a stolen card or two, hacking a travel site, doing something to save us some money. But we played it straight. We didn't even take anything from the hotel, not even the pens in the room, or the slippers they give you for free. We lived like honest men for a week, taking a total break from our usual lives. Well, almost.

Frank still read all the time, his philosophers, you know, concentrating on the Italian thinkers, Marcus Aurelius, Giambattista Vico, Antonio Rosmini-Serbati, and Benedetto Croce. He even brought along a copy of *The Annals* by Tacitus. "Location as organizing principle," Frank said, admiring his small stack of books. He read and read and read some more. And when he wasn't reading, he talked about what he had read, and if we were back at the hotel room he talked with the TV turned up loud in the local language. "You can learn a little of the language," he said. I never learned anything. It was almost like being deaf for me, like not hearing anything.

There was an old British couple who sat at the table next to us at dinner at the hotel. They were just retired, not that old, I guess, but old-school. They dressed for dinner, with him in a suit and tie and her done up with jewelry and makeup and her hair properly set. We were out on the patio, our tables overlooking the sea, with the small waves flashing silver against the nighttime sea. The beach was still crowded, even at night. Tourists trudged up and down the steps leading to and from the parking lots, the sand, the sea. They came and went with no consequence. It was all at a safe distance. Everything was quiet and tranquil. And then the Brit spoke.

"This is what I like," he said, "sitting at a table and watching people go by. It does something to your outlook on life."

Frank and I nodded but didn't say anything to encourage him. We watched the waves, the lights off in the distance. Frank closed his eyes and held his face up to catch a warm breeze.

"It comes up from Africa," the man said. "It will be hotter tomorrow."

He introduced himself and his wife and launched into what he knew about the weather and the town and the hotel. He and his wife had been coming to the same hotel for almost thirty years. They come the same week every year. He liked to talk, and we let him. We heard about the changes in the hotel, which weren't that many, over the years, and the changes in guests, which were mostly regrettable. "They try to sort them out," the man said, "but I guess some of the odd sorts always slip through." Frank gave the man a long look, but we didn't take his meaning the same way. He smiled and the wife smiled and he went on and told us about their favorite places, that sort of thing.

"There's a tennis court not far from here. Do you play?" I told him I was on the team in high school. Frank gave me a look. It was a lie and a mistake; I knew that. But we were on vacation. I wanted to give the man something. And now he had it and wouldn't let go. "Did you bring your kit?" he wanted to know. I hadn't, I told him. I hadn't played in years. "Too bad," he said. "I'd love to get in a game with you." It was a detail he kept for every time he saw me the rest of the trip. "I've asked about a racquet," he told me at breakfast.

"I don't have the right shoes," I told him. "Besides, I wouldn't give you a good game."

“Any game is a good one,” he said and again lamented my lack of kit.

Frank wanted to avoid them, but they were nice enough. Our schedules seemed to align with theirs – we saw them at breakfast and at dinner in the hotel – and I didn’t want to change our schedule, so we continued to see them. He talked about tennis and previous trips, and she was mostly quiet, and all we had to do was listen for a few minutes. They had a charm about them, and seemed to know every shop, restaurant, and doorway in the area. They were fixtures of a sort, a reminder of what the world used to be like, when people used to make their way on the Grand Tour, I imagined. “Colonialism,” Frank said.

They had told us their names the first night we met them, of course, and if we had known that we would see them every day, some times multiple times in the day, we would have made an effort to memorize them, but we carelessly rejected them as needless information, and now we had seen them too often to ask them again. We were familiar to them and we had to act as if they were friends. We were not friends. We didn’t know each other. We began to call them Mr. and Mrs. Brit, Frank and I, but only to each other. We didn’t know what to call them to their faces, so we resorted to formalities, “sir” and “ma’am,” which we hoped they would accept as respect and not a moronic cover. It must have worked, as they seemed to gravitate toward us at dinner and breakfast, always sitting at the next table. And every morning he mentioned tennis, and commented on my absent skills. “You really need to play,” he said. Mr. Brit never came to breakfast in his tennis gear. She was equally dressed, in summer dresses or slacks that always seemed to elevate the room. She knew what to wear and probably laid out his clothes for him. She had fine, modest jewelry, except a vintage Cartier Tank watch, gold with diamonds, that Frank spotted immediately. “That’s a thirty-thousand-dollar watch,” he said. “Easy.” I gave him a look, the one he liked to use. “Just a professional observation,” Frank said.

IIIII

The wind came from Africa, just like Mr. Brit said it would and we were quickly done with the heat and the blowing sand on the beach and decided to take a boat ride. We stood on line for the ferry, or what passes for one in Italy, on the wide stone pier, the sun searing above us, and the heat radiating off the stones from below. We felt like Shadrach and Meshach when Abednego and his bride, Mr. and Mrs. Brit, appeared out of the throng, happy to see us. We were dripping with sweat, in swim trunks and t-shirts, while Mr. Brit appeared cool and dry in a crisp linen blazer and trousers. Mrs. Brit was in white linen slacks and starched cotton shirt with a wide-brimmed summer hat. Her Cartier was clasped over the left cuff of her shirt.

The ferry was a double-decked boat and Frank and I debated whether to sit above in the heat and the sun, or below in the heat and shade. "What's the chances of it being air-conditioned?" Frank said. The air conditioner at the hotel barely worked and when Frank complained to the staff, they shrugged and said nothing could be done. "The Italians hate it," Mr. Brit said. "But they don't seem to be bothered by the heat like some." Frank swears Mr. Brit took a disapproving glance at our sweaty t-shirts, but I don't think so. "I know where to sit," Mr. Brit said. "Stick with us."

The ferry held about four hundred, and it seemed as if about twice that many people were standing on line, but when the time came to board, not that many left the pier. Mr. and Mrs. Brit led us to the left side of the upper deck, so we would have a better view of the coast, and in the shadow of the pilothouse, so we'd be out of the sun. We sat on aluminum benches, with Frank across from Mr. Brit and me across from his wife. "It beats the bus," Mr. Brit said. He was absolutely right, until it went wrong.

We were on our way down the coast when the boat suddenly stopped. We didn't know if they had cut off the engines or if they had gone out on their own, but we bobbed in the sea a hundred yards or so from the rocky shore. We sat there for fifteen minutes or more, with the boat bobbing around in the waves and the sun beating on the deck and the wind coming up from Africa. A couple of people got sick, throwing up over the side of the boat. "We've never seen this," Mr. Brit said. Frank got a book out of his bag.

Mr. Brit took notice of the book and took it right out of Frank's hands. "Tacitus!" he said and looked at the pages Frank was reading and began to read aloud. "In general, a black and shameful period lies before me." He closed the book and looked at Frank. "Don't read this book," Mr. Brit said. "It is poison. I know Tacitus. In my college days he came near souring me into cynicism. I have long been of opinion that these classics are the bane of colleges. But Tacitus – he is the most extraordinary example of a heretic; not one iota of confidence in his kind. Without confidence himself, Tacitus destroys it in all his readers. Drop Tacitus. Come now, let me throw the book overboard." Frank reached for his book, but Mr. Brit pulled it closer to himself, almost teasing Frank with it. "This book," he said, "will you let me drown it for you?"

"Don't," Mrs. Brit said to her husband in a way someone scolds their dog. She took the book from Mr. Brit and handed it back to Frank. With her left hand, the one wrapped by the Cartier watch. Frank noticed it again and thanked her for the book.

Mr. Brit and Frank engaged in a dueling sulk; Frank returned to Tacitus, holding it up in weak defiance, while Mr. Brit refused to look in our direction, staring off toward a place where no one ever read or ever heard of Tacitus. Mrs. Brit gave me a conspiratorial smile, amused at her husband's uncharacteristic wounded silence. We were still stranded, with no explanation from anyone and no visible sign that anyone was working the problem. The rocky coastline bobbed up and down in the distance, the cars snaked their way along the road above us, boats passed by with little more than curiosity.

"They'll send another boat," Mrs. Brit said to me. Her husband didn't respond, but continued to look elsewhere. Then, the engines started again, sputtering back to life, and we continued on as before. "That's better," Mr. Brit said to the wind or the water or the coast, before finally turning back to his wife. She reached for him with her left hand and took his right hand and held it, coaxing him back to his old self. It wasn't long before he began talking, telling us about this or that thing on our left, the town up ahead. Frank put his book down and nodded at Mr. Brit's observations, but I should have known that the skirmish might have ended, but there was a battle waiting to be waged.

We all got off the ferry in Amalfi and Mrs. Brit offered to buy us lunch without saying it was an apology for her husband. "There's no need," I said, "besides, we're not dressed for it." "Then at least let us buy you a drink," she said and was needlessly embarrassed when I told her that we didn't drink. "Well, that's that," Mr. Brit said. "We'll see you at dinner then," Mrs. Brit said and I assured her she would.

We wandered along the crowded side streets, basically wasting time and avoiding anywhere we might see Mr. and Mrs. Brit. Frank wouldn't even take the ferry back. "Never get on the boat," Frank joked. "It's never get *out of* the boat," I corrected him. "Not in this movie." We took a bus back. We didn't even get seats and had to stand in the aisle and try not to fall over as the bus wound its way around every sharp turn. The air conditioning was feeble at best, and the inside of the bus smelled like stale sweat. We were contributors; our t-shirts soaked from the heat and the exertion of staying upright in the aisle. What had been an almost idyllic vacation was literally being shaken and we thought the best thing to do was to get back to the hotel as soon as possible.

We showered and took a long nap. By the time we got back up the sun was going down. We didn't stay in the hotel for dinner, but walked down the road and had pizza at an outdoor table with a view of the sea.

"It's still beautiful," Frank said. "As long as you don't leave."

"If we didn't want crowds, we shouldn't have come to a place that's crowded," I said.

"It's fine. Tomorrow will be better. Just remember, never get on the boat," Frank said.

When I woke up the next morning, Frank was gone, and by the time I made it to breakfast, he was finished and sitting on the patio looking over the beach and out at the sea. The wind had shifted. Gray clouds scraped across the tops of the cliffs, bringing cooler weather but no rain. The sea was rough, too rough for the smaller boats. Tacitus waited on the patio table, next to Frank's empty coffee cup. "You were sleeping," Frank said. I went and got a plate from the buffet, the usual fruit and cheese and a pile of small pastries. I rejoined Frank at his table. The waiter brought a cappuccino and Frank ordered a second.

"Another couple of days," I said. "Maybe the weather will hold."

"Let's not go to Capri today," Frank said, changing our plans.

"Okay." That was fine by me. I didn't need to go anywhere, and definitely didn't need to get on another boat for a while.

I ordered another coffee and glanced at my watch. "Mr. and Mrs. Brit are quite late this morning," I said. Frank didn't respond. Or he did, by returning to his Tacitus. I sat and waited, waited for the sun to burn off the clouds, waited for Frank to figure out what we wanted to do, not really caring if we did anything at all, waited in the way we had waited the previous days, for the day to take its natural course and we didn't worry about anything, nowhere to go, no job to do, nothing to accomplish. “It’s called relaxing,” Frank had said.

Mr. and Mrs. Brit arrived just before breakfast service was over. They were not relaxed. They were still properly attired, but noticeably agitated. They filled their plates and sat next to us, and Mrs. Brit seemed hesitant, as if she wanted to tell us something but was thinking better of it. “We thought we were going to miss you this morning,” I said.

“We’ve had something of a morning,” Mrs. Brit said and her husband seemed resigned that the story would be told.

“Never had anything like it,” he said. “Not here anyway.”

“Maybe I misplaced it like you said,” Mrs. Brit said.

“I’m having more confidence in your version of things,” he said. “If you said you put it in the safe, you put it in the safe.”

“My watch is missing,” Mrs. Brit said. “I know I put it in the safe last night. I always do.”

“They have these safes, but how safe are they? They must have a master combination or key to them. Someone took the bloody thing.”

“The only thing missing,” Mrs. Brit said.

“Stolen,” he said. “They knew what to take and what to leave behind.”

“I don’t know why they didn’t take it all,” she said.

“You’ve talked to the police?” I said.

“We did, but they’re not much help are they,” Mr. Brit said. “The watch is probably in a pawn shop in Naples by now.”

“You never know,” Frank said. “It might show up.”

“It’s not a stray cat trying to find its way home,” Mr. Brit said. “It’s in someone else’s pocket.”

“You have to have confidence,” Frank said, and then I knew. I knew where the watch had gone and where it would go. I didn’t say anything. By the afternoon, the watch had been found, back in the Brits’ safe, exactly where they said it hadn’t been.

“You can make the watch appear and disappear all you want,” I told

Frank, "but don't throw Tacitus at him. Even I caught that. He'll figure it out." Frank didn't say anything, never admitted anything to me, never explained or apologized, or changed. I thought he'd get caught, that Mr. Brit had to know that Frank had taunted him. But he didn't. The watch came and went one more time, right before we left. One last message from Frank to Mr. Brit, or maybe to me, or both. Frank knew what he was doing, but that didn't mean he couldn't get caught. Prison is full of people who know what they're doing. I wondered what an Italian prison would be like.

The Brits checked out, moved to a different hotel, and Frank said he wished we were staying longer. When we were on the plane leaving Italy, I half-expected to see the Cartier on Frank's wrist, but that wasn't his way. "It all turned out all right, in the end," he said. "See, my confidence wasn't destroyed."

11

THE EXIT

THE MINUTE I OPENED MY EYES I KNEW HE WAS GONE. The room was dark and quiet, nothing seemed out of the ordinary, but I could tell the bed was half-empty, that the room was different, that Frank wasn't in it. I tried not to think about it for a second. I tried to tell myself that he had gone to get the car so we could get out as soon as possible. But I knew it wasn't true. I stayed in bed for a minute. The room was the same color as the inside of my eyelids. I opened and closed them a few times. Exactly the same color. I couldn't tell the difference. I wanted to wait but knew there would be no point. Nothing would change. I turned on a light and went to the closet. All of Frank's things were gone. The bag for Froehmer was gone.

I had half-suspected this day would come, had half-waited for it, but I always thought it would be because of something I'd done, a mistake he couldn't forgive. I never imagined what it would be, maybe nothing at all, just some sense of him walking out the door instead of putting up with me anymore. But I'd always imagined it would be our door, that he would walk out of our home, leaving me there, not some hotel room in a strange city. I always thought it would be my fault; I never thought Frank would steal, not from me.

I texted Frank, knowing he wouldn't reply. "Call me. Let me know everything's all right." I called and left a message. I texted again. I called again. And the more I did it the more distance I could feel between us. After a while I got dressed and packed my bag but didn't go anywhere. Maybe he'd still come back. I knew it wasn't true. I stood in the room for a long time, not knowing what to do; I stood still going a hundred miles an hour, like an engine with the gas and the brakes both pushed to the floor, frantically trying to figure out what to do. I had to do something. So, against my better judgment, I left the room and went to the lobby. That was worse, the bright empty space made me feel like I was on stage, being watched. It was starting to get light outside. I went out to the sidewalk, the last place where I waited for Frank and he had come. So I went out. Frank wasn't there, but the fucking horse was back, lying there in the street as if it had never left. I had walked out of the room and stepped into a nightmare.

2

12
FRANK

"PEOPLE THINK THE WORLD DOESN'T MAKE SENSE," FRANK TOLD ME NOT LONG AFTER WE MET, "ONLY BECAUSE IT ISN'T THE WORLD THEY WANT. If you're looking for fairness or justice, then it might seem to make no sense, but if you look at it as an indifferent machine, then it makes complete sense. It's an indifferent, cruel, fucked-up world, but it makes perfect sense. It's like a slot machine. You sit there and plug money into it for hours, coin after coin, and get nothing back. You give up and some guy comes right up to the same machine and puts one coin in and hits the jackpot. Is that fair? No one expects it to be. It's not bad luck or good luck or fate; it's just random action and no one questions the randomness of it, the unfairness of it. Everyone knows it's not fair. But everybody has to play, and everybody has to keep on playing, and the more you play, even if you hit a jackpot or two, even if you go on an amazing winning streak, the more you play, the more you lose. And in the end, the machine has taken everything you have. That's the way the universe works."

I met him in rehab. He was leading a reading group. A greatest hits of Western philosophy, more or less. I remember the first thing I heard him say: "Socrates says that the unexamined life isn't worth living; Sartre says the examined life isn't worth living. I say they're both wrong. Every life is worth living." I almost walked out right then, but it was better than a lot of the other crap they tell you in rehab, and Frank's class got better, after a while.

"I'm not here to justify your life," Frank said, "and the things you've done in it. But I'm here to justify you being alive and, I hope, introduce you to people who think about what that means."

I tried not to think about it. I knew where I was and what I'd done to get there. And who I owed for helping me. Froehmer was paying for my treatment. "What do you think your dad would do?" he asked.

"I'd be on my own, in jail for all he'd care."

"Well, I'm not doing this for your dad; I'm doing this for you."

It wasn't cheap, and I knew Froehmer wasn't doing it for free. I'd be back swiping stuff from construction sites and industrial parks and city garages and wherever else he wanted as soon as I got out. And I didn't care. What else was I going to do? I didn't need Socrates and Sartre and Frank to help me with any of that. At least that's how I thought. I only wanted a distraction from all the other stuff that went on, group sessions and counseling, talking and more talking. At least Frank would have us reading something and talking about something other than ourselves.

Frank's seven years older than I am; he'd been to college and had worked a lot of different jobs. He worked on a server farm at some big tech firm, worked packing boxes at a warehouse for an online retail company, installed alarm systems for a while, worked as a landscaper, a handyman, pushed a broom as a janitor, painted houses, jobs like that, one after another, never staying with any of it for long. "I'd get high and not show up for work," he said, "sometimes for days. And I'd just not go back. Or I'd get caught stealing. I got fired a lot."

"What did you steal?"

"Anything I could grab quick and sell quick. I didn't care, anything that would give me a little cash to get high again."

"Jail?"

"Once. Usually they wouldn't know for sure that it was me. Or, I should say, they would know for sure, but they couldn't prove it. So I mostly got bounced on my ass all over the place. I wouldn't recommend it, but at least I'm well-traveled, occupation-wise anyway."

"What do you want to do?"

"As little as possible," he said. "Like what I'm doing now. Teach a little, travel a little, read a lot. How about you?"

"I've only had one real job, I guess. Been only one place. Haven't read much at all."

"What was the one job?"

"Inventory management and personal procurement specialist, I'd guess you'd call it." We'd known each other enough that I wanted to tell him.

"Personal?"

"Someone tells me what they want and I go and get it."

"How do they find you?"

"Not directly. I've got a go-between. He calls me and tells me what to get. I never know who it's for."

"Ever been caught?"

"Not yet."

"You going back to it?"

"Just long enough to repay the guy who helped me out here," I said.

"How long will that take?"

"I'm not sure. A few years, I suppose. Longer than I want, I know that."

"Would it go faster with two?"

"I don't know about that. It would make it seem faster, anyway. But I'm not asking for help."

"You know what a SafeTight 4000 is?"

"No."

"You might need some help," Frank said and went quiet.

"You're not going to tell me."

"Tell you what?"

"What the SafeThing is?"

"It's one of the most popular home alarm systems around. The control panel to be exact. You've never seen one?"

"I don't go that route. I have other ways to get what I'm after."

"You never know though, when that kind of knowledge can be put to use."

IIIII

I was almost out of treatment, almost ready to leave, and Frank was worried about what was going to happen. The only thing I was worried about was where I was going to go. I had everything else covered, I thought. I'd work for Froehmer, I'd still see Frank, I'd stay clean. Everything would be all right. "You should still go to meetings," Frank said.

"I'm going to tell you something that maybe I shouldn't," I said. "I'm not an addict." I'd been saying I was for almost three months, but I never believed it. “I’m dependent on things, but I’m not addicted to them. I don’t need the meetings.”

“You can’t go back to your old life and think you’re not going to fall into the old routines, the old ways of doing things.”

“There is no old life,” I said. “I’m a different person now. You know that. I took drugs to be someone else, to feel like someone else, but I know who I am now. I like who I am. You taught me that.”

“It’s not as easy as you think,” Frank said.

“It will be easy for me,” I said. “Watch me.”

“I will,” Frank said and I had a place to stay.

IIIII

Frank had a small one-bedroom apartment when I moved in. There was a mattress on a metal frame and a nightstand and lamp in the bedroom and a chair in the living room. And books everywhere. “I still have more than I need,” Frank said.

“Anything in the cupboards?” I asked.

“Plenty.” He had dishes and pots and pans – all of which he knew how to use – and food on the shelves and in the refrigerator. “I don’t like to go out much,” he said. So we didn’t. We did get another chair. And a few months later we bought a couch, which I took as a major victory and Frank took as a cause of concern. “I don’t want a lot of clutter,” said the man who had books strewn all over the place.

“Not a lot,” I said, “just enough to make it look like someone lives here.”

Frank came to his aversion to things from books, a philosophy cobbled together from a variety of sources, distilled down to what was useful for him, sort of the way, Thomas Jefferson cut out the parts of the Bible and the Koran he didn’t agree with or find necessary. I came to my aversion through experience. I didn’t want anything because I’d already had everything taken from me once. I wasn't going to let them take anything again. And if I didn't have anything, there was nothing to take, nothing to lose. One thing treatment teaches you is how to do without. You deny yourself the things you want most, the feeling you get from the drugs, the drugs that give you the feeling, the want itself. You do without today and then you worry about tomorrow when it comes. You do without every day until the want goes away, which it rarely does. Or not for long. Most people can't deny the want, can't do without, and they relapse. There's no shame in it, but I didn't think it would happen to us. Frank and I could do without. Maybe taking other things helped us with that, I don't know. I let Frank think about that. And what he thought, he put into practice. "We don't have too little," he liked to say, "Everybody else has too much."

IIIII

"I've got a partner now," I told Froehmer.

"What's he do for you?" Froehmer said.

Frank and I had been working together for about six months before I said anything. He'd come along on the first few just to watch, to see if he could add anything to the equation. He sat and studied the target the same as I did, but he saw things I didn't. "They have a dog walker," he said while we were watching a house. I saw the dog in the window, but didn't think much about it. "How do you know?" I said. Frank shrugged. "Wait," he said. A few minutes later a woman showed up with three dogs in tow. She walked up the stairs and opened the door and emerged with the waiting dog added to her pack. "Same time every day, more or less," Frank said.

"How do you know they don't have cameras inside?" Frank wanted to know.

"I don't care," I told him. "I'm only inside for a few minutes, not long enough for anyone to do much about it, even if they see me. Besides,

I have this." I showed him a stocking cap I always put on once inside, pulled down over my face.

"And how about security systems?"

"In and out before the cops can get here."

"Safes?"

"I don't mess with them. If I can't find what I'm looking for, I leave."

"And you've never been caught?"

"Not once," I said.

"You've been lucky," Frank said. "And you're lucky you found me."

That's when Frank rigged up his toolkit. He could sweep for cameras, mess with them when he needed, get by security, and even break into a few cheap safes when needed.

"He extends our expertise," I told Froehmer. I'd come up empty-handed a few times for Froehmer, either not being able to find what he sent me for, or, more often the case, not being able to get inside. Froehmer never complained and never criticized. He would only say, "You did all you could, right?" and that would be that. I only got paid on delivery, so Froehmer wasn't out anything if I didn't deliver. I always assumed Froehmer got what he wanted some other way, with someone else's help. "We can take on more work."

"I give you what I have," Froehmer said, but we did get more jobs.

"His cut comes out of your end," Froehmer said, but after a few of the more difficult jobs he sent our way, my cut went up. Froehmer didn't say anything about it. The only thing he said was, "Just remember, the more parts a machine has, the more things can go wrong."

I always expected to get caught, either through some fault of my own, or just due to the law of averages, but once Frank joined, I started to think maybe every job would be flawless. Frank had that way of solving the problems. You didn't think anything would go wrong; you didn't think chance would ever enter into it.

IIIII

Frank never met Froehmer, never wanted to. "He's your guy," he said, "besides, he doesn't need to know both of us, does he?" Frank didn't want anyone in his life he didn't invite in, and as far as I could tell, that included hardly anyone but me. I never met any of his family; he never even talked about them. He had friends, I'm sure, but I never met any of them. Frank could build walls around different parts of himself, keep his life in different compartments. Maybe that's why he never wanted to meet Froehmer. But I think the main reason was that Frank still had a foot in the respectable part of the world. He still volunteered at the treatment facility, still had a strong connection to the staff and the patients, and still had a need to share things with them, teach them a thing or two from his books. He'd been a sponsor to a lot of people, and as far as I could tell he still was. He was on the phone a lot every day, trying to help this or that person. He never talked about any of them with me, not in any specific way, but he did all he could to help a lot of people.

"Sometimes you gotta give back," Frank said, not as explanation but as expectation.

"It's easy for you," I said. "You're smart. You're good with people. They like you, listen to you, all that. I got nothing to give."

"Time," Frank said. "You can give that. That's all they need. That's what I give them, really. Everything else is for me. Believe me, I take more than I ever give."

In the end he took everything.

13
THE BAR

IT'S HARD TO SIT ALONE AT A BAR AND NOT HATE YOURSELF. I sort of feel that's why they were built the way they are, a long line of sturdy wood to accommodate a row of people, who all feel alone, even if they're with someone else, and a big mirror right there in front of them to remind them how truly alone and miserable they are. I was miserable enough, but I wanted the reminder.

I hadn't started out there. I left the empty hotel room and the horse in the street and went to the diner where we'd gone only a couple of days before but now seemed years ago. I sat around there for a while before I couldn't take it and had to go somewhere else, somewhere we'd never been. I called Frank again. I texted him again. I called the rental car place. I called all the rental car places. I called the bus station. I didn't call Froehmer. I sat in the diner and watched it fill up with people heading off to work, rushing in and out as if the world couldn't wait for them, as if they made a difference in the world. I sat and looked at my phone over and over until I had to put it in my pocket. I couldn't sit there anymore, in the sound of people hurrying, knowing exactly where they were going and what they were going to do. I didn't know. All I knew was that I had to get out of there, so I walked around, back to the hotel. The horse was gone. I went back to the room and lasted there only a couple of minutes before I had to leave again.

I had wandered around and then wandered into the nearest bar that was open. It wasn't even noon yet. Frank was gone and I didn't know what to do or where to go or what to tell Froehmer. I had to tell him something. I had to do something. I had to figure it out. I was going to sit around anyway, so why not sit around in a bar, where that's what they expect you to do?

There were maybe five people in the place, and the two women at the end of the bar looked at me with disapproval. A thick guidebook was on the bar between them and they passed a phrase book back and forth. They spoke Italian to each other and tried to speak English to the bartender, who stood near them, ignoring me. I couldn't hear what they were saying, and probably wouldn't have wanted to anyway.

I was the only guy in the place, and had clearly, unwittingly entered a lesbian bar. I didn't care. I only wanted a place to think, and I didn't want to go to a diner. The two Italian lesbians at the bar were dressed alike, in blue jeans and matching gray hoodies. They had short black hair and dark eyes that kept returning to me. They didn't look alike, despite their best efforts. They knew what I looked like, though;

they were noticing everything about me. I thought about leaving, but I stayed put and looked at the bartender every now and then. Finally she came over.

"Tourists," she said. I tried not to take it personally.

"Coffee," I said.

She poured a cup and put it in front of me. "I don't know how good it is," she said. "Let me know. I can put another pot on." She didn't wait for an answer and moved back to the end of the bar to the Italians.

I looked at the coffee, a small dark pond in a white cup, and tried to think about Frank the way Frank would think about him, if he were a problem that needed to be solved. Why would he leave? I wasn't even sure that was the right question. I went over everything, from Frank getting back to the hotel, to the accident, to me handing the statue to Frank. There had to be something in there that made him leave. I remembered him saying the statue wasn't worth anything. That statement was either true or false. The statue either had value or it didn't. If it did, was it worth enough for Frank to take off on his own with it? It obviously was worth something, or else we wouldn't have taken it, but it couldn't be worth that much, not in actual value. Not to Frank, not to anyone other than the person who wanted Froehmer to get it for them. So, if it wasn't worth a lot, why did he leave with it? We'd stolen a lot of things that would be worth more money to someone else, that Frank could have taken and sold somewhere, easy and clear. So why this thing? Was that even the right question?

The bartender came back. She poured a little more coffee in my mug. "Everything all right?" she said. I nodded. "You sure you're in the right place?"

"I'm meeting someone," I said. She gave me a kind of encouraging shrug with her mouth and glanced at her watch as she left me again.

The girls showed her pictures from the guidebook, which was as big as a stack of Bibles, and the bartender nodded and tried to make herself understood.

I checked my phone for the hundredth time and took another look into the coffee. I had to tell Froehmer something. He wanted to know when we were delivering. I couldn't ignore him much longer. I was hoping I could find Frank before I had to lie to Froehmer. I was sure I could find Frank; I only needed to think about it a little longer. I could figure things out when I needed to. Frank would always know where to find me, but could I find him if he didn't want to be found? Maybe I hadn't started at the beginning; maybe I hadn't gone back far enough. Maybe it all had to do with that goddam horse. Maybe that's why Frank left. He had figured that out, he said. He never told me what it was all about. I was way behind. I drank coffee and watched the girls. We left each other alone.

There were rows and rows of bottles behind the bar. I didn't care. I looked at the coffee and I looked at the bar. It was impressive, twenty feet of oak, a lot more than a hundred years old, I bet. Impressive enough to warrant a page in any good guidebook. Depending on the manufacturer and the condition on the parts I couldn't see, the bar could be worth as much as twenty thousand. I wondered if anyone else in the place had any idea of the value of the thing.

When I used to spend my time drinking there was a dive I used to frequent that had a Brunswick from around 1880 that still had the metal trough attached to the bottom rail. There was an ongoing argument as to whether it was a spittoon or a urinal. "They spat in it and maybe scraped their boots, but that's it," the bartender said, "but it wasn't a urinal." "No plumbing," one of the regulars said, "and no women. Why wouldn't they take a piss in the thing?" Every new customer started the argument all over again. I don't think anyone ever wanted to figure it out. There'd be one less thing to talk about. The dive is gone now. The bar is gone, stolen for a song by someone who knew what it was worth, from someone who had no idea. And I'm stuck with coffee and lesbians and sitting in front of twenty thousand dollars that isn't going anywhere.

I'd been staring at the cold cup of coffee for more than an hour. The tourists had taken their guidebook and were off to see the sights, and the bar was still there, and the mirror, and the miserable loneliness. The bartender came back around even though she knew I didn't need anything, not anything she could give me anyway.

"You think she's still coming?"

"He knows where to find me," I said. "But I don't know how to find him."

"That's the way it always works, isn't it?" she said. "Stay as long as you want. Let me know if I can help."

|||||

By the time I got back to the hotel it was late afternoon. I'd stayed at the bar as long as I could, waiting for Frank to find me, waiting for Frank to contact me, waiting to figure out what had happened and where he was, waiting to think of something to say to Froehmer. None of it happened. I finally texted Froehmer that we wouldn't be back until tomorrow. He never replied. When I got to the hotel, I understood why. He was waiting for me.

The elevator doors were about to close when an arm sent them back the other way. There were three other people in the car, none of whom looked too pleased that their ride was held up by a couple of seconds. Froehmer stepped into the car and didn't acknowledge me at all. He stood silently across the car, then gave me a hard look. I stared straight ahead, watching the lights in the elevator. There were two stops before my floor and I didn't know what to say to Froehmer when the time came. The car stopped and the doors opened and I walked down the hall to my room. Froehmer lagged behind me and I could practically feel his anger pressing against me, like the heat from a stove. I stopped at the door to my room and waited for him. He kept his distance and kept his eyes on me. "Everything all right?" he said.

"Everything's all right," I said.

"Where's your partner?" He never said his name, always called him "partner."

"He should be here soon."

"Should we wait for him?" Froehmer said and motioned for me to open the door.

There was no point in me continuing to lie to him. I either had the thing for him or I didn't, and if I didn't I'd have to tell him where it was. We went into the room and Froehmer looked around. He could see the made bed, the empty bathroom, the empty closet. He sat down and waited for me to say something.

"I don't know where Frank is, and he has the thing, but I'm sure I'll hear from him soon. I just need more time."

"When did you last hear from him?"

"This morning," I said.

"He had the thing with him then?"

"He took it after," I said. "But he'll be back with it."

"Don't be so sure," Froehmer said.

"What can he do with it, anyway?"

"He can fuck things up," Froehmer said. "And he's doing a good job of it."

"There's an explanation," I said. "You'll get what we came for."

"You'll make it right."

"I will."

Froehmer stood up and I knew he wouldn't hit me or anything – he wasn't that type of man – but I wasn't sure. Maybe when he was younger, back in college, he could have taken me. Maybe he still could, but I could hold my own, I thought, if he tried something now. I was afraid of him, but I wasn't afraid of fighting him, if I had to. "You stole from me," he said. "You might think that your partner stole something from you, but really, you stole from me. So you need to do right in this. You need to make this right. Understand?"

I understood. I was on the hook for Frank and what he took. Froehmer left and I stayed standing where he left me, not knowing what to do. Not one idea. I texted Frank again. I called and left another message. There was no point to any of that. There was no point to anything until I heard from him, or could figure out where he'd gone.

IIIII

I stayed in the room and tried not to look at the phone every five seconds. I tried to read; I tried to watch TV, but nothing could break through. The gears in my brain had seized, grinding together over and over without being able to move forward. The whole thing made me so anxious I was almost vibrating, shaking with frustration, dread and indecision and ignorance. I was going to go crazy in that room. I thought about going back to the bar; I thought about going to any bar, but it was just a thought. I knew where that would lead, farther from where I needed to be.

In the end, I went to the rental place and got a car and drove home. Maybe there was an answer there. The car was as big and lonely as the black, starless sky. It had been almost twenty-four hours since I last saw Frank. In the five years we'd been together I don't think we went anywhere close to that long apart. We were together all the time. I tried not to think about it, but there's nothing lonelier than a long drive in a half-empty car, except a long night in a half-empty bed.

It was almost three in the morning by the time I got back to our apartment. Our car was still parked in the same spot. I wondered if Frank would have taken it if we'd had it with us on the job, if Froehmer hadn't insisted on us using the rental. I walked into the apartment and knew no one had been there. Nothing had changed. Everything was where we had left it, Frank's clothes in the closet, his toothbrush next to mine, his copy of *Meditations* open and page down right where he left it. His saxophone was in the living room. Everything was all exactly where we had left it, and maybe it would all stay there. It seemed impossible that he would leave everything, with no explanation, but I thought that if he hadn't come back by now, he wouldn't be coming back ever. All of a sudden it didn't feel like home. Maybe Frank really wasn't coming back. There were no answers anywhere, none that I could see.

I woke up well after noon. I was still tired and could have stayed in bed another week or more. But I didn't. I checked my phone and made a few calls and then found a meeting. I didn't go every day, but enough that people knew me, even more knew Frank. He still talked to a few people whenever they needed someone to talk to, and they always needed someone to talk to. No one knew anything about Frank. A few of them had tried to reach him but hadn't heard anything either.

"Trouble in paradise?" someone snided at me and I ignored it. I didn't know what to say to them, how much to tell anyone. These weren't my friends. But it was my community.

"It's easy to look after people you like," Frank had told me. "It's another thing to care about people you don't like."

Most of them cared about me; all of them cared about Frank.

"I haven't heard from him in a couple of days," I said. "It's not like him, that's all."

Everyone agreed. It wasn't like him. I didn't think he was the type to turn his back on everything, to walk out of his world without a word, without an explanation. But maybe he was exactly that type. Maybe that was the only way he could do it. They tell you in treatment that you can't go back to your old life, because you'll go back to your old habits, so maybe that's what Frank did, changed everything.

I don't remember much about the meeting – they're all about the same, the same confessions, the same conversations, the same crap food and crap coffee – except a woman who got up near the beginning and talked. She was about my age, maybe a little older. She'd lost her daughter to social services because of her behavior. She'd hurt a lot of people, "more than I ever hurt myself," she said. But she was sober now, today, and trying to put her life back together. She felt good, not in the immediate post-rehab euphoria, but in the longer, steadier satisfaction of being clean and clear, contributing instead of constantly taking. "I know you're not supposed to say 'I got this,'" she said. "I know you're not supposed to say it, because the minute you think you've got this disease all put to bed, it comes right back. But I have to say, I feel good. Today. Today I've got this. I've been clean one hundred and eighty days today and I've never said it before, and maybe I won't say it tomorrow. But today I can say it. I've got this." She got a big applause and I clapped too, but I was thinking about Frank. Those were the words he said when I got out of the car. I hadn't thought about it before.

I didn't really buy into all the therapy and meetings and everything else they try to sell you about recovery. But Frank did. I suppose it's easy to dismiss all the structure and support they offer; I had Frank to look out for me almost every minute of every day. If I felt like using again, he was right there. But, as I've said, I never really considered myself to be an addict. It's not that I wasn't tempted into going back to alcohol and drugs, but for me it was always an easy choice. It's different for an addict. An addict has about as much control over their choices as a hemophiliac has control over a nosebleed.

"The world is a trap," Frank liked to say, "and the better you understand how the trap is made, the better you can avoid it." He liked to tell the people he helped that the world was designed to create addicts; they create a stressful environment and then insist you buy the relief from the stress, whether it's alcohol, sex, TV, food, drugs, shopping. Binge watching, binge eating, binge shopping, all of it marketed and celebrated, and then denigrated for those who get addicted to it.

"They set the traps, and then blame you for getting caught," Frank would say. Frank believed it. He believed that the world worked a certain way, but he also believed in uncertainty. You didn't know what was going to happen tomorrow, but you could plan for it. Maybe he believed it because he was superstitious, maybe he was superstitious because he believed it. I think he wanted so much control in his life because he was always worried about the next trap. Maybe he finally got caught in one. Spending too much time at meetings can make you an amateur psychotherapist. I didn't need that. I needed to be an amateur sleuth. And I figured that Frank had never come back home, and wouldn't. He was still in the city somewhere, and I needed to get back there.

14
THE POOL

I WAS STILL ON MY LATE-NIGHT ROUTINE; I CHECKED INTO A HOTEL SOMETIME AFTER MIDNIGHT. I wanted a hotel with a pool, and the minute I stepped into the lobby I knew they had an indoor one. I thought of the comedian who says that by the smell of it you don't know if the hotel has an indoor pool or is trying to cover up a murder. Maybe it's the way he tells it. The guy checking me in didn't think it was funny. He'd heard it all before; I was counting on it.

I had wanted a hotel with a pool; I wanted to be around water. I would have been better off filling the sink in the bathroom and sitting next to it. When I woke up, I grabbed a coffee and followed the smell of chlorine. Three kids were tormenting each other in the pool – two sisters and a brother, splashing and teasing and ratting each other out to the parents, who couldn't muster more than a quiet "behave yourself" and then went back to ignoring them, the way people ignore yapping dogs. The parents sat in chairs next to the water, clearly hoping to get the kids out and onto museums, a tour bus or two, something the kids would hate. They'd be happy spending the day splashing around in the pool, and for a while I thought they might.

I slumped in a chair at the opposite end of the pool from the parents, knowing full well that I looked like a creep in full attire, shoes and socks, pants, shirt and jacket. I pulled my cap close to my eyes and tried to see only the water, just look at it for a while and think about what to do next. The water slapped against the sides of the pool as the kids thrashed and splashed around, and the sound bounced around inside the glass partitions that tried to keep the whole thing part of and apart from the rest of the hotel. The kids were between eight and twelve, cranked out in quick succession when the parents were young enough for all the trouble. The boy was the youngest, but would have been outmatched if it had been the other way around. He tried when he could to get at his sisters, picking at them when he thought his parents weren't looking. The kids stayed in the shallow end. They were as white as string. Underwater they almost glowed with a ghostly fluorescence. None of us belonged there.

I tried not to pay attention, but the kids started fighting over something; the boy had it and the girls wanted it. "Give it back," one of them said, and the parents parroted it. The boy sheepishly held it out in his hand (it was too far away for me to see), but somehow – through his own deviousness or incompetence – it fell from his hand and went to the bottom of the pool. There was a brief dispute as to who was going to fetch it; the young boy seemed reluctant to dive down the few feet and retrieve it. Maybe he couldn't. Finally, one of the girls swam down and brought it back. This became a new game. The father took whatever it was that started the thing, then tossed coins into the pool, and the kids chased after them. Except for the boy. He never went under, even when his sisters gently coaxed him. Instead, he sat on one of the steps in the shallow end, squatting down so he was underwater up to his chin. His sisters would bring him the coins and he'd toss them back, farther out into the deeper water.

"That's far enough," the father said, but the girls kept diving down and getting the coins. I didn't think the father had anything to worry about; I doubted that the boy could throw the coins far enough to get to the deep end of the pool, but he tried. After his father told him far enough another time, he flung them with all his strength, all at once. A couple of the coins made it into the water, but a few hit the side of the pool and rolled around on the concrete deck. The girls dived and retrieved the coins and the father ordered his son to go and find the ones that rolled. The boy had no idea where to look. No one helped him. They all stood at the other end, watching him search in vain.

Finally, the father told him to forget it. "Let's go," the father said. I had watched one of the coins and knew exactly where it was. I got out of my chair and went and picked it up and handed it to the boy, along with another coin I had in my pocket. The boy didn't even say thanks. He ran back to his father and proudly showed him the coins in his open hand. The father took the money and put it in his pocket. The mother draped a towel over her son's shoulders and they left. I had wanted to be alone, but now that they were gone, I didn't want to be by the pool. I felt like more of a creep now than before.

I sat and looked at the empty pool for a while more and I figured out what to do. Or at least where to begin. If Frank was still in the city, like I thought he was, I thought I knew what he was doing. Or at least what he'd done.

IIIII

I drove back to the target house. I watched for a while until I knew no one was home. I got out of the car and walked down the street. I walked back and went directly to the back door. The window was still unlocked. Who leaves a window unlocked after they've been robbed? Most people lock everything up tight after the fact, after it would have done some good. Everybody does what they should have done, long after it would have mattered. I went back to the car and watched the house some more. The son came home from school and disappeared inside. The mother came home a few hours later, and the husband an hour after that. I watched until all the lights went out, then I went and got some takeout Chinese and drove back and watched some more.

I'd been gone about twenty minutes, enough time for someone to leave the house, enough time for someone to go in and out again; it was an uncertainty that would bother Frank, bedevil him (and me) to the point where, if Frank was adamant enough, or persuasive enough, we'd have to try to determine what had happened in the gap.

"You can't proceed if you don't know," Frank would argue.

He was right, but I was confident nothing had happened. I ate the food and wondered if I would regret it, regret taking my eyes off of the place for even twenty minutes. I had a hunch I had to play. If I was right, twenty minutes wouldn't matter. Twenty hours wouldn't matter. There was a bed waiting with no one in it (a couple of them, in fact), and a pool I'd paid for, stinking the place up with chlorine. But I didn't need it. I stayed put and watched.

I had a hunch, but I had Frank's logic in my head too. I had to keep an eye out. I had to be sure. I finished off the food too early. I put the empty cartons back in the bag and put it in the back seat. I didn't even crack the fortune cookies.

I watched the house until the sun came up; I watched it until everyone left, first the father, then the mother and son. I watched after they left, sitting there in our car, watching it the way we had a few days ago. But it was only me, and I wasn't exactly sure what I was going to find when I went inside. I knew what I wanted to find. If my hunch was wrong, I wasn't sure what I was going to do.

So I waited. I waited, longer than I needed. Finally, I returned to the window by the back stoop and went inside. I was up the stairs and into the office in less than thirty seconds. I knew when I entered the room; I knew I was right. The goat trophy was sitting on the shelf, just where I'd found it before. Frank hadn't run off with the thing; he'd brought it back. I heard the voice echoing from the pool, "give it back." Frank gave it back. And I was going to take it again, finish the job. I would give it to Froehmer. The job would be done. At least that would be settled. It didn't explain where Frank went, or why.

Only I didn't take it. It was sitting right there and I left it. Maybe because Frank had put it there, maybe he knew what he was doing. Or maybe I was afraid. I don't know. I don't know why I didn't take it when I had the chance. I should have. If I had, everything from then forward would have been different. You can't start thinking like that though. If you start thinking about one thing you could change in your life, or would have done different, you might as well start thinking about all of it. I would have never got mixed up with Froehmer, would have never had him take care of my problems, I would have never started stealing, but then it wouldn't be my life and I would have never met Frank.

IIIII

I left empty-handed, a hunch confirmed, and went back to the hotel and sat on the bed and tried to think it out, at least a couple of steps ahead of what I was doing. I wasn't good at this part. I texted Frank. "Everything ok. Everything. Ok?" I didn't expect to get an answer and I didn't. Frank would turn up when he decided he could. I figured his superstition got the better of him. He was waiting for the gears to mesh again before coming back. He had made everything right, had put everything back in place, and now needed things to reboot. That's what I figured anyway. One hunch had paid off; I was hoping for another.

15
THE BREAK

FRANK HAD LEFT ONCE BEFORE, BUT NOT FOR LONG. It was early in our partnership, maybe the tenth or twentieth job we did together. We were sitting outside the target house, eating Chinese food when I handed Frank a fortune cookie.

"Don't open it yet," he told me, but it was too late.

"Then don't read it," he said.

I didn't take him seriously.

"It's a good one," I told him.

"I don't want to know," he said and put his cookie up on the dash so I could see. He started a scan of the house, looking at the network, any security system, and his usual stuff.

"Fuck," he said, "we can't do this."

"What's going on?"

"I know this guy," he said. "He was in treatment."

"You're not supposed to ID the guy," I told him. He didn't say anything. "Maybe it's a different guy."

"It's not a different guy. It's because you opened the cookie."

I laughed at him.

"I'm serious," he said.

"No, you're not."

"Maybe we should be."

"Maybe we should just do the job."

"Maybe," Frank said. "But maybe not. Not with me, anyway. Not this one."

And he got out of the car and I didn't see him for a couple of days. I texted him, called him, but nothing. I remember being worried that he was using again, but it wasn't true. He called and told me he was back at the treatment facility.

"I just need to think things through," he said.

"I didn't do the job," I told him.

"That must have made Froehmer happy."

"I told him I knew the guy. He told me we'd be doing the next one for free."

"It all worked out," Frank said.

"You can still go to meetings," I told him. "You don't have to change anything."

"It's already changed," he said. "For the better. But I miss being part of this, you know."

"You can still do it. I can take care of this end."

Frank came back, but it wasn't the same.

He worked days – like a normal person – at the center, and by the time he was done, I was usually gone. We lived in different hemispheres of time; we shared the same space but rarely saw each other. It was almost like living alone, but there was enough evidence of him – a book left on the table, a shirt thrown across the bed, maybe a note left for me on the kitchen counter – to make me miss him. As if I didn't miss him all the time.

I went to the job on my own, the way that I had before Frank, but it might as well have been my first time. I wasn't quite sure what to do, or how to do it. I'd already forgotten how to work alone. Frank and I had quickly forged a true partnership, already developed an almost seamless way of working together, and the things I had done by myself before now seemed more complicated, more troublesome, and the things that Frank did, the things he was teaching me, I struggled with, couldn't quite remember how to do them, or was afraid I was doing them all wrong.

My confidence was failing; my capabilities were down by half. I tried to tell myself that I knew what I was doing; I'd done it all just fine without him and I would be fine without him in the future, but it didn't seem that way, not on the first time out, not on the fifth, not on the fifteenth. I had given him part of the job, and now I couldn't take it back, not as easily as I thought. I would look for him in the passenger seat, hoping for help, hoping for advice, or just some conversation to get through the dragging minutes of the heavy hours of sitting. But he wasn't there.

IIIII

One night I sat in the car, struggling to focus on the target house, my mind wandering across the mistakes of my past, wondering if I'd made another one. I hadn't thought about Frank ever leaving, but I wondered if he would again. Why would he stay? I thought, if he was going to go, it was better now than later. He could go back to his life at the clinic and whatever else he did, and I hoped I could go back to mine. I wondered if it could be that easy. I wasn't smart enough to know the answer. I wondered if I was smart at all. I thought about a line from Hunter Thompson, "in a world of thieves, the only final sin is stupidity." I didn't know if it was true, and I know I hadn't shown many smarts at the important stuff of life, but I'd been sure about Frank. I convinced myself that he had it figured out, and I wasn't going to like the way he'd figured it.

Things went on like that for another week, almost two, each of us living in those separate spheres that rarely intersected. Somehow I didn't screw up anything, still delivered for Froehmer, but I became convinced it was only a matter of time before I fucked up in a big way. I hated the dread I dragged around, my drifting thoughts that only reinforced my doubts. I didn't have time to wait for it to pass. Something had to be done.

IIIII

I called Froehmer and told him I wanted out. Well, not entirely. I told him that I wanted to go back to construction work. He told me to meet him at the diner.

I met him in the parking lot, but we didn't go in. Instead, I got in the back seat and we drove around. Froehmer was in the front passenger seat, and his guy Mobley drove. He was almost a mascot, like a family pet you're used to seeing in the same place, a dog curled in the corner that you know will bite sooner or later.

It was like a bad version of *On the Waterfront*, and Mobley looked like a low-rent Charley Malloy. Only I wasn't his brother, and he didn't do any of the talking. Froehmer did most of that, telling me what a good job I was doing, even with the one incomplete, which he brought up more than twice, holding it over me like it hadn't been repaid. I kept as quiet as Mobley and listened until he was done with the compliments and complaints. Then I told him again that maybe it would be better if I went back to the construction sites.

"Where's this coming from?" he said. "You, or your friend?"

"I think I can be better help to you if I go back where I was."

"It would be better for me if you stayed where you are," he said. "But I leave it to you. It's a step back, though, you know that."

"I don't see it that way."

"You should start seeing it that way."

Mobley didn't say anything, but I could see him watching me in the rearview mirror. He was trying to tell me something, the way he was staring at me, but I didn't pay attention. I was surprised he didn't wreck the car, as much as he had his eyes on me.

"I need you to make the most out of this arrangement," Froehmer said. "the way your dad always did. I want what's best for you, the way he would've wanted it. And I think it works best the way we're going, for now. But I'm willing to make changes if you're willing to help me out first."

"I'll do what I can."

"I know you will. I need you to do two jobs for me, two small jobs, and then, after that, if you still want to go back to construction work, that's what we'll do. How about that?"

I agreed and Mobley drove us back to the diner parking lot, right where we'd started.

IIIII

Froehmer had sent me to get some soldiers. Twelve of them, and their horses. They were lead toys, all ready to go in a red cardboard box sitting on a coffee table in some guy's den. I sat around and watched the house for a couple of days, the usual deal. All I had to do was walk in and get the box and walk out, but the guy had a lot of toys. Alarms, cameras, and other sophisticated gizmos, on the perimeter, around the windows and doors, and some inside. I wasn't sure I could disable them or get around them on my own. That was Frank's adeptness. I did what I could but wasn't sure I had done enough. I texted Frank and gave him a list of the tech I could identify on the house.

I didn't hear back.

I didn't have time to wait. I thought I had disabled the alarms, scrambled the cameras, interrupted the wifi, and a few other tricks Frank had tried to teach me. Some of the devices would only be offline for a few minutes. I had done things in the wrong order, I knew that. I should have texted Frank before I started pulling the plugs. Now I had to go. So I went.

It took me a few minutes to get inside, longer than I could afford. Luckily, the box was right there in the open. I ran to the den, grabbed it, and got the hell out of the house, convinced that cameras had come back online. I told myself not to care; they wouldn't find me. They wouldn't see my bland face; they wouldn't know who I was. I was gone.

I got back to the car, and there was Frank, sitting in the driver's seat, holding a bag of Chinese takeout. I took the food and he drove.

"I knew you didn't need my help," Frank said.

He glanced at the box and said, "That's a good twenty-thousand-dollar box of toys."

"I needed your help," I reminded him. "I needed you. I'm shocked I got out of there, that's how much I needed you. Let's get this box to Froehmer before the cops get to us."

"Let's give him the food instead."

We could hear sirens in the distance. They were getting closer.

"It's not for you," Frank said.

"A couple more jobs and Froehmer will let me out."

"You think he's going to let you out? You really think that?"

"He has to. If I want out, I'll be out."

"Do you?"

"I don't want things like this."

Frank waited for the sirens to fade.

"I'm ready to get back in," he said.

I wondered if Frank only came back because he knew Froehmer would never keep his end of the deal, that there would always be another job. "You're too good of an earner," Froehmer had said. Maybe Frank knew I'd get caught sooner or later without him. Maybe I never really wanted to stop in the first place. Maybe Frank knew that too. I didn't really care; he was back. And we could go on, better than before.

16
THE CALL

"FRANK SHOWED UP," FROEHMER SAID OVER THE PHONE.

"With the thing?"

"No," he said and I knew it was no good.

"He never made it back," he said.

"What does that mean?"

"I got a call," Froehmer said. "Frank OD'd. I'm sorry about that."

"Where? When?"

"Not long after he left you, I guess. Took the thing and sold it and bought enough stuff to drop a couple of Philip Seymour Hoffmans."

I didn't correct him. I wasn't thinking about that. I just wanted Froehmer to keep talking, to tell me what I didn't want to know.

"Where is he?"

Maybe he said "morgue," I don't really remember. I know he was oddly direct and oddly vague at the same time. "Never left the city. Got his fix and another hotel room, they told me."

"Who told you?"

Froehmer knew people. Somebody who knew somebody, maybe. Froehmer knew how to find things. Then he had me go and get them.

"I want to go see him. Take care of things. I'll go get him."

"Already taken care of," Froehmer said. "Not a good idea to go see him. Wait for the funeral. Come on back. If you need something, let me know. But come on back." He was worried. I could hear it. I wanted to tell him not to worry about me, but I wasn't sure myself. You never know how someone is going to react to the news. Besides, I wasn't going to go back, not yet. I was going to see Frank. I didn't care what Froehmer said about that.

Somebody had to go see him, to stand over him the way they do in the movies. I'd stood over my father, watched him die in the hospital and stood over him after they pronounced him dead. "I'm sorry for your loss," the nurse said after she took the stethoscope from his chest and turned off the machines and wrote down an official time. "Sorry for your loss," she said and left me alone with him. I stood and looked at my father and thought how young he was, but how much older he was than my mother. I'd stood and looked down at everyone I'd ever loved. And now I was looking at Frank. They had him under the name he'd used for the job, not his own but the one on the driver's license and credit cards he had in his pocket. It was stupidly comforting; I could pretend it wasn't him. For a little while anyway. As long as it wasn't Frank I didn't have to think about how none of it made sense.

They led me down the hallway and into a stainless-steel room and it didn't make sense. I don't mean in the sense of justice, the way the world works, how the way things should be get fucked over by the way they turn out. I mean, something was wrong. I knew it the minute I saw him. Something wasn't right about it. For one, his arm was a mess, bruised and scratched and cut, like he'd shot up with a rake. Like he didn't know what he was doing. A user doesn't forget how to use. Besides, when did Frank not know how to do something? Frank didn't overdose, not by himself, anyway. Somebody gave him the shot, and somebody gave Froehmer the wrong story. I thought about calling him right away to set him straight, then I thought better of it. He wouldn't be happy that I saw Frank in the first place. I'd talk to him later about who told him about Frank, who gave him the story. Froehmer could find out who was responsible. All he had to do was find them; I would go get them. Frank didn't do this. It was someone else. It still didn't make sense.

|||||

The morning after my mother died, I heard her in the kitchen making breakfast. I was in my bed and I could hear her, like every other morning, cutting fruit or mixing waffle batter or making scrambled eggs, something good to get me out the door and off to school. I knew she wasn't there, but I heard her all the same, heard the familiar sounds she used to make, and could smell something cooking on the stove. When I got downstairs, it was my father at the stove. He was carefully cutting a leftover baked potato, cutting it into thin slices and placing them in the hot pan. He then took a couple of pieces of sausage and cut them into thin slices and added them to the potato. Finally, he took some eggs and added them in the same pan. I had never seen my father make breakfast. He would grill a steak or a hamburger, maybe even some chicken once in a while, but I'd never seen him in the kitchen at breakfast. He was usually up and gone by the time I got up.

|||||

I sat at the table and watched him carefully orchestrate his meal. He had bread in the toaster and placed a couple of plates next to the stove. He poured some coffee and quietly set the cup in front of me and returned to the stove. He had the eggs and sausage and potatoes plated just as the toast popped. He buttered the toast and put the plate in front of me and carried the other with him to his seat at the end of the table. He looked at the plate and then at me. "I don't know how we got through yesterday," he said, "and I don't know if we'll get through tomorrow, but I know somehow we'll get through today." Then we ate.

When my father died I made that same meal, and repeated the same lines to myself. When Frank died, I stayed in bed. I didn't want to eat; I didn't want to get out of bed; I didn't want to get through the day; I didn't want tomorrow to come. Finally, in the afternoon, I went down to a coffee shop and sat and drank coffee.

The place was busy with a steady stream of people coming and going, and a number of people parked at tables, staring into their phones, their computers, whatever was in front of them. No one was paying any attention to anything.

There was a woman sitting at a table by herself. She had her computer in front of her and her phone next to the computer. She took off her watch and set it next to the phone. She would stare at her computer for a few minutes, then check her watch, then check her phone. It irritated me. And the more she did it, the more irritated I was. A thousand other days I would have thought about it for a second and moved on, but on that day it stuck to me like a nettle and I got stuck on watching her and getting more and more annoyed. Frank was gone and this woman was still taking up space. She had a clock on her computer, and another on her phone, but she had to keep checking her watch. I couldn't stop looking at her; I wanted to go over and scream at her. I thought about leaving, just to get away from her, but I kept sitting there and after a while she got up to go back to the counter. She left everything on the table.

I got up and walked past and pocketed the watch and left. I hadn't made it twenty feet out the door when the woman stopped me. She was with one of the workers, who looked eager to be part of the confrontation.

"You took my watch," she said.

"What?"

"You took my watch," she said.

"You're wrong," I said. "I didn't take anything." I opened my jacket and said, "Go ahead and check for yourself." She hesitated. "Go ahead," I said, as calmly as I could, the way Frank would have said it. I turned to the employee. "You want to check?" He didn't know what to do. "I saw you take it," he said. "Then go ahead and check. Or do you want to call a cop?" I said, "We can do it that way too."

"We'll call the cops," the woman said.

We all went back inside. A few people were staring at us, but mostly they went about their own business. The employee went to call the police. I walked back to the table and turned and said, "I was sitting here. Where were you?" The woman motioned to her things, still in place on the table.

"You were twenty feet away from me," I said. There was someone at my table so I moved closer to the woman's table. She backed away from me as I approached. "Relax," I told her. "Look at where you were and look where I was. I couldn't have taken it."

The employee was back from his call. "You took it when you walked past," he said. "I saw you."

"You saw me? From behind the counter? Could you go back and show me." He walked back behind the counter and I walked to the woman's table. "What was I doing?" I asked.

He wasn't sure now. "I saw you," he said but he wasn't as eager as before.

"Okay," I said. "We'll wait for the cops. Where do you want me?" The employee motioned for me to move near the cash register, so someone could keep an eye on me, I suppose. The woman went back to her table and looked out the window, waiting for help. Finally, someone saw it. A guy got up from his table and walked behind the woman and said, "Is that your watch?" and pointed to it on the floor, pinned against the wall. I'd let it fall down my pant leg a good ten minutes earlier. No one was paying attention.

The woman was confused, and the employee was struggling to square what he knew he'd seen with what he now saw. He apologized, but the woman didn't say anything. I should have taken my luck and left, but I was still annoyed, more at myself now than anyone. I launched into the woman, yelling at her about false accusations and how if she'd kept better track of her stuff, she wouldn't blame other people. I might have yelled at her about how no one needs a watch anymore anyway. "What would I do with a watch? What would anyone do with a watch?" It might have gone something like that. I was half out of my head, suddenly becoming the person I was before I met Frank, I thought. I finished my rant and calmed down.

"It's all right," I told the woman. "But you'll have some explaining to do with the cops." I left before they got there. Taking the watch was supposed to be my small tribute to Frank, I told myself, and I'd almost fucked it up. If they hadn't been worse than I was, they would have had me. They never should have let me go back inside, and nowhere near the woman's table. And I should have planned better, studied the room, seen all the angles. I wasn't Frank. I'd gotten through most of my life on my own, and now I wasn't sure I could get through any more of it without him. I had barely passed the first test. I went back to bed.

IIIII

I arrived as early as possible to the funeral home for the visitation, thinking I'd be the first one there, but there were three other people already sitting with Frank. It was a husband and wife and their daughter and I knew right away it was Frank's family, the one I never knew he had. His father looked the way Frank would have looked thirty years from now, and his younger sister had his same pleasant face, with softer features that held a brightness that had not been dulled yet.

The sister got up and walked across the room to greet me. She lacked the calm confidence Frank always had, there was a fragility about her; she looked like chipped glass. “You must be Rick,” she said. “I’ve heard a lot about you. I’m Casey.” She leaned in and gave me a brief hug. “My parents don’t know,” she whispered and walked me back to meet her mother and father. “This is a good friend of Frank’s,” she said.

“How do you know Frank?” the mother wanted to know.

“We met at the center,” I told her. “He helped me through a lot. Helped me all the way.”

“You stayed in touch?”

“Every day,” I said. “He was always there for me. All the time.”

“It was a terrible choice he made,” the mother said.

“It was an awful disease,” I said and let it drop when I saw her face harden with disagreement.

“Well, thanks for everything you did for Frank,” Casey said. She motioned for me to sit next to her and I did. I tried not to look at Frank lying there next to us. There were a lot of flowers in the room, all with white envelopes attached. Casey noticed me looking at them.

“You should read the notes,” she said, “they’re all nice, nice tributes to Frank.”

I couldn’t look at them.

“He helped a lot of people,” Casey said.

“He hurt a few too,” her father said.

It’s the hurt that lasts.

|||||

Hundreds of people came to the visitation. Almost all of them told his parents and sister the same thing, how much Frank had helped them, what a good person he was, how much of a difference he’d made. All I could think is that they didn’t really know Frank. They knew part of him, a version of him, but not the complete person. Maybe that's all I knew too. Maybe that's all we can ever know about each other. Maybe I don't even know what I'm talking about. But I know that the version they found of him was not the version I knew. He died with someone else's name and someone else's drugs. I certainly didn't know that person. I was at a stranger's wake.

Frank's father acted as if he were at someone else's service too. He casually picked at his fingernails, checked his watch, checked his phone. He was running out the clock. I tried not to judge. Everyone deals with grief in their own way. I remember how calm my father was at my mother's funeral. He sat and shook hands and listened as everyone said something meaningless and sympathetic. My father nodded and thanked everyone for coming. His voice never wavered; he never cried. Everyone talked about how strong he was. "You're a rock," they told him. "Be strong for your son. He needs you to be strong." Except he wasn't strong. He was the weakest I'd ever seen him, too weak to cry, too weak to do anything at all except sit there and endure it. He had been emptied out to a brittle shell, and afterward, what filled him was bitter. It took him a long time to regain his strength, only to have it taken away again in the end. I told myself that I wouldn't be like my father; I wouldn't be weak. I had to have strength to figure out what happened to Frank. I had to have that or I would have nothing.

Out of the hundreds of people who came to see Frank all laid out at the front of the room, I recognized a couple dozen. We hugged and cried and I didn't tell them anything, as bad as I wanted to. It was better to keep it all to myself, until I knew more. For all I knew the person who was with Frank when he died was in the room. It had to be someone he knew, I thought. The room was full of addicts. The closest I came to explaining anything was with the man who ran the rehab center.

"Where were you when it happened?" he wanted to know.

"Asleep," I told him. "We'd been down in the city for a couple of days. I woke up and Frank was gone."

"Anything happen out of the ordinary?"

I shook my head and then changed my mind. I would tell him one thing. "We were in a fender bender, nothing bad."

"Sometimes that's enough," he said. "Or maybe it has nothing to do with it. It's hard to tell sometimes. Sometimes you never know."

IIIII

I tried not to look at Frank, but he always seemed to be in the corner of my eye. People approached, usually coming from taking a look at him, and Frank would be there in the background, lying there in the coffin. I didn't want to see that. I didn't want to know anything about it. Froehmer had taken care of it, just like he said he would, but I was left with the thought that Frank was going to be buried in someone else's clothes.

My father couldn't pick out clothes for my mother, he couldn't even look at her things, couldn't open her closet, so I had to pick her burial outfit. I picked out my favorites, the things I remembered her wearing the most around the house, I guess, a pair of jeans and a black watch flannel shirt. It's what she changed into whenever she got home; it was her go-to clothes and I figured it's what she would have wanted to wear. My father didn't care; he didn't even want to know. At the last minute he decided he couldn't bear looking at her at all and had a closed casket. I could still see her lying there in her go-to clothes. It's what she's always wearing whenever I think about her. It was easier with my father. He only had one suit. I took it down to the funeral home and handed it off with a white shirt and a tie and that was that. It didn't dawn on me until later that I had worn that suit to my senior prom. I lost my virginity wearing that suit, or not wearing it, rather. I'm not sure it was worn after that until my father needed it one last time. Now it has pockets full of cash, and a young man who could still teach me a few things. No one would put any cash in Frank's borrowed pockets, but he still had things to teach too. I needed them all, my parents and Frank, but they were gone and I had to learn to do without. You learn it and learn it until you're left with nothing but the learning.

I tried not to think about it. I looked for Froehmer, but he didn't come to the visitation. I wanted to thank him for everything; I wanted Casey to meet him. He had never met Frank, never laid eyes on him as far as I knew, but he had taken care of everything, just like he said he would. More likely, it was someone who worked for him, but he had done it all, and then never showed, the same way he never showed at my father's funeral.

IIIII

But he did show. The next day, Froehmer slipped into the funeral once the service had started and took a seat behind me. I was sitting behind Casey. The first pew had just the family, Casey and her parents, all dressed in black. The mother seemed small in her black dress, a tiny cinder left at the end. The father flipped through the hymnal or some other book. Casey hugged me and motioned for me to sit behind her. It was straight church, with hymns, and readings and the Book of Common Prayer. I stood when everyone else stood and knelt when everyone else knelt, and read along with the prayers and the hymns, but I kept my mouth shut. The words meant nothing to me. I wished they did. I can see how they might bring comfort to somebody, the idea that they've left us for some place better, a mansion, the priest said, but I didn't believe it. The priest talked about the death of Lazarus and how Jesus said that anyone who believed in him would not die, but then Jesus goes and raises Lazarus from the dead. All I could wonder why Jesus didn't raise everyone from the dead, then. Why didn't he raise Frank from that box? If death meant nothing, why was Lazarus brought back after four days in the tomb? It was just a story, just like the thieves on the cross and all the rest of it. It meant nothing to me; they're just stories. They may have power over the others, but it doesn't work on me. They might be afraid of pain and punishment in the afterlife, or heaven and all that, but if I do something wrong, I want to pay for it in my own way. That's all I could think about as we went down to our knees and back up again and the words and more words came and went, and Frank stayed there in the front, barely mentioned in the whole service.

A lot of people talked at my father's funeral. That's what he wanted. He didn't want any stiff sermons and dropping to your knees every few minutes. He wanted stories about better times and drinking after a short service. "Just enough to get me in the door," he told me. Guys talked about what a tough boss he was, but how he wouldn't have anyone do anything he wouldn't do himself. "He had me go around a job site and pick up all the unused brick," Pete Tejada said, a smile already creasing his face. The masons always left bricks at the job site. My father had them picked up and stacked so they could be used again, instead of carted off and used on some other job. "So, I'm out there, just a kid trying to make an easy buck" (which got a good laugh), "cursing this guy who's making me walk around picking up trash bricks, when I see him behind me, picking up half bricks. I look at him and he holds one up and he says, 'I got to pick up twice as many to keep up with you.' He outworked me every day," Pete said. "And always had a smile on his face." There were a lot of stories like that about my father. There weren't any about Frank, at least none said at the front of the church where everyone could hear. Except from Casey.

At the end, the priest acknowledged that he didn't know Frank, so had his sister come up and talk about her brother. She talked about the hurt he had caused in his life and the struggles he tried to put behind him. "Addiction is a disease that affects more than just the addict," she said. "It affects everyone the addict comes in contact with, family, friends, colleagues, everybody. It's like a rock that gets thrown in the water and the ripples go out and out. Frank told me that. He knew the ripples he had caused, the damage his behavior had done not only to himself, but to everyone he knew. That's why when he got sober he tried to be a different kind of rock, to create different ripples. He wasn't part of my life for a long time, too long, but we had reconnected not long ago," she said. "We talked at least once a week and texted more than that. He was in a good place, I thought, better than he'd been in a long time, maybe better than he'd ever been. Maybe it wasn't enough. There are people here who know him better than I do. Maybe you know different than I do. All I know is that he wasn't always a good person, but he was trying to be a better one. You can't ask for much more from someone."

The mother stared at Casey and when she looked back at her mother, Casey got choked up. The father wasn't looking at anything. Casey was going to say something else, but decided against it and came back to the pew. The priest brought the service to an awkward end and invited everyone to stay for coffee and cake. Some people came over to Casey and introduced themselves, telling her how Frank had helped them, how he helped a lot of people, how happy he seemed, how much good he did. I sat there and then realized that Froehmer was gone. You couldn't blame him. The service had turned into a meeting. Frank would have hated it, I'm sure. I left too.

I walked out to the parking lot, to wait for the procession to the cemetery. Froehmer was standing by a car talking on the phone. I waited for him to finish, then joined him. "I couldn't take it anymore," I said.

"They said a lot of nice things."

"They always say a lot of nice things about the dead. They rarely say the truth."

"What would you say?"

"I didn't say anything. I won't say anything. I learned that from my father. And you."

Froehmer nodded and leaned against the car. "I'm sorry for you. I'm sorry for Frank," he said. "He thought he had it figured out."

"He had it beat," I said. "He had it."

"You have to know who's in charge," Froehmer said. "You have to respect it. That's what got him in trouble."

What did Froehmer know about it? He didn't know what he was talking about. That's what people who don't know anything about addiction say. "I don't know," I said. "Something's not right about it."

"The whole thing's not right," he said. "Some people aren't made out for this. You are. He should have listened to you. Not the other way. I should have done more. Maybe I could have helped."

"You did all you could. More than you had to."

"I didn't do anything," he said.

"I want to make things right," I said. "I want to finish the job."

"It's taken care of."

"Let me get the thing like we planned. Let me get it for you."

"It's taken care of."

"You found it?"

"We know where it is," Froehmer said.

"I can go get it. Let me."

"Don't worry about it. Take some time. There will be another job."

"Let me make things right," I said.

Froehmer studied my face for a moment, probably seeing how much it meant to me. "Okay," he said. "You've got it. But wait for my go ahead."

17 THE SISTER

SHE TOUCHED EVERYTHING HE HAD. She picked up every shoe, every sock, ran her fingers through his shirts, put her hands in the pocket of his pants, made sure to inspect each and every thing he owned like a blind person might. She cradled his saxophone like an infant. She picked up a book Frank had on his nightstand, *Moral Actions and Their Relation to Modern Law*. "This is my brother's," Casey said. "Yes it is," I told her. "You have the same tastes?"

"Not really," she said. "A shared interest, I guess. But I didn't have to read everything, you know. He'd tell me about it all anyway. I didn't have to read. I got the summary and the dissertation."

She examined the back copy on the book and said, "Maybe I should give this a try."

"Not that one," I said. "I read that. Spoiler alert: moral acts are still a threat to the State. If Jesus were alive today maybe he wouldn't be crucified, but he'd be locked up in a maximum security prison. That's the gist of it."

"That much progress in twenty-one centuries?"

"Is that progress?" I took the book from her and held onto it. If she had opened it, she would have seen Frank's handwriting in the margins. He had used that particular book to try and rationalize what we did. He didn't have a problem with stealing, not usually, but he had a problem with hurting other people. He occasionally needed to sort through it all, and wrote comments in the book as he worked through his arguments and defenses. "People shouldn't put value in things," he wrote. "Theft can be a moral action, not Robin Hood, but a more existential act. No one owns anything, it all simply passes through our hands." I don't know if I believed any of that, but I knew it wouldn't get us very far with the law.

I didn't have the same problems and qualms that Frank had, but I couldn't help him sort any of it out for himself. I could only listen, could only listen as he read from the book and read the things he'd jotted down, wishing he hadn't put any of it in writing. I put the book in a drawer of my things, hoping Casey would forget about it.

She was over at the closet, studying his shirts. She had asked to come over. Her parents had gone home. I let her stand around the apartment and touch as much stuff as she wanted, for as long as she wanted. "Can I take a shirt?" she said.

"You can take anything you want. You can take as much as you want. You can take everything if you want."

"I couldn't do that," she said. "You'll want to keep something."

"I don't know if I can."

"You think that now, but you'll see. But don't get rid of anything. Please don't get rid of a single thing. You can always get rid of it, but you can never get it back. You know?"

"I know," I said.

"I'll take a few shirts," she said. "I make bears out of them. I volunteer at a group. We give stuffed bears to families who want them when they've lost someone to addiction. They make a request and give us the clothes and we make them a bear. Look." She showed me a few pictures. It's just what it sounds like. "I thought I'd make one for myself and one for my parents. I could make you one?"

"I don't think I could look at it."

"People find them surprisingly comforting," she said. "We've made almost two hundred. I'll take an extra shirt, just in case."

"That's okay," I said.

She stood at the closet, a shirtsleeve hanging between her fingers, and it hit her. It comes in waves, big and small, and it's not always the big ones that get you. "I started making them because of Frank, you know. He was always talking about giving back when I told him I wanted to help. I started because of him," she said through the sobs. "I never thought I'd be making one for him." It was a big wave; it got the both of us.

"We hadn't been in touch in a long time," Casey said. "It's only the past few years. After he'd been with you a while, I guess. He was happy, he said. Everything was good for him, he said, maybe for the first time. Did he ever tell you about us?"

"Not a word."

She laughed but not because it was funny. "I'm not surprised. There was a lot of hurt there. He never got along with our parents. He figured out early on that he was smarter, that they were holding him back. But it got bad in college, then worse after that. He started using in college. Not experimenting, the way some people do, but exploring. That's how he described it. He was using to try to figure himself out. And he liked the version of him on drugs best of all. He had discovered something, he said. It was all from stuff he was reading, you know. Right? He thought he had it under control. He would never be an addict, he told me. We argued about it, but he had it all figured out.

"He got a job teaching high school. And he confided to a group of students about this discovery he'd made about himself. And that led to someone telling someone else until the school had to investigate. He got fired. It's the only job he ever cared about. He was born to teach, you know? But no one would hire him, so he went from job to job, only working to keep his habit going, until the habit got bigger than the job, then he started stealing and getting caught and getting fired. Then he started stealing from my parents, then our grandparents. My grandmother found him hiding under her bed, trying to make off with her jewelry. She called the cops on him and my father refused to let anyone post bail for him. He detoxed in jail.

"He started using again as soon as he got out, just to spite our dad, I think, to prove he was still in control. He wasn't in control, but he hadn't found bottom yet. Bottom was a long way down. We had nothing to do with him, not even when he went into rehab the first time. Not when he was almost dead in the hospital. And then when he got clean, he didn't want anything to do with us. Then he reached out. He's been in a real good place. I never would have thought . . ."

"He wasn't always good," she said after a while. "But he was better, wasn't he?"

"For a long time," I said. "When did you hear from him last?"

"When you were down in the city," Casey said. "He said you were down there and told me where you were staying and I remember I said, 'is it because of the horse?' And he got real excited. 'What do you know about the horse?' he said. I told him that everybody knows about it. 'Tell me,' he said. I told him that some guy has an old circus horse that comes and lies down in the street in front of the hotel sometimes. 'The woman at the hotel said she didn't know anything about it,' he said. 'She's probably just tired of talking about it,' I told him. 'It's in all the guidebooks.' He started laughing, laughing really hard. He said it had been bothering him. 'You don't even know what hotel you're staying in,' I said. He laughed some more. He said you were going to laugh too."

"He wouldn't do anything until he figured it out," I said. "And it's true about the hotel. They acted stupid about the whole thing."

Casey laughed. "Frank had his superstitions, didn't he?"

"Always?"

"Only after he was clean. I'm not even sure they're superstitions. He had to know how everything was, you know, had to see all the pieces on the board, so he could try to figure out his next move."

"That's right."

"You think he saw this move?" Casey said.

"Did you?"

"I know enough to know that you never know what's going to get someone off the wagon, but I would never have seen this coming. He was in a good place. I'm telling you. He talked about traveling, the two of you going off somewhere, Greece or Italy. He was looking forward." She paused and gave it another thought. "That doesn't mean anything, though. You know that. There are a lot of people who look forward and still fall back, you know."

"I know," I said, "but I don't know if that was Frank. I'm not convinced of that."

"You have to let that go," she said.

I couldn't look at her. I couldn't let it go, and I couldn't let her think that about her brother. “What if I told you that I don’t believe he took that shot himself?”

I didn’t want to tell her. I don’t know why I did. I’m usually better about keeping my mouth shut. She shook her head, not wanting to hear, but I kept talking anyway. “I saw him,” I said. “I saw him after they’d brought him in. His arm looked like a pin cushion. He didn’t do that to himself. Someone else had been jabbing at him.”

“Who?”

“That’s what I’m going to find out.”

“You want me to help.”

“No,” I said. “That’s not why I’m telling you. I just needed to tell someone, you know. The person I would usually tell, well, you know. Besides, I’m not sure where to start with any of it.”

“Well, you know what Frank would say.” I knew. She said it anyway. “Start with what you know and go from there.” It was good to be reminded.

18 THE THING

FRANK WASN'T TALKING. He stood in the hotel room, looking at the images on the muted television, but not watching them. He didn't want to talk.

"What's the dumbest thing we ever took," I said, trying to get him out of it, away from his own head.

"None of its dumb," he said, "not to the people who want the stuff." Then he thought about it. "But it's all dumb, if you think about it long enough."

"But the dumbest. I mean, we stole a houseplant once."

"That houseplant was worth twelve thousand dollars," Frank said.

"You don't want to talk about it."

"I want it out of our hands as soon as possible," he said.

"We could drive back tonight. Rent a car somewhere else. If that's what you want. Give it to Froehmer first thing in the morning."

"It's all right," Frank said.

"What about the car?"

Frank shrugged. "Just some guy not paying attention. He's got all the information. The rental's got all the information. None of it leads back to us."

"Or Froehmer?"

"Or Froehmer. It's all taken care of. Nothing to worry about."

He wasn't worried. He was just somewhere else. He wanted to be somewhere else. I didn't give it much more thought than that.

And then, sometime when I was asleep, he left. Took the thing and went. That's what I knew. That's where it started.

19
THE KNOWN

I SPENT DAYS ON THE PHONE. Froehmer had said they found Frank in another hotel. So I started calling. I started with the credit cards I knew he had on him. He had three of them that I knew of. Actually, he had five, but two of them were still at home, on the desk in front of me. I ended up calling them too, trying to see if there was any activity, any information about where he'd gone and what he'd done. There were five different names, a different identity for each card. I called and went through the automated prompts, for once grateful for the lifeless voice on the other end. There were no current charges. Then I started calling the hotels, using the names on the cards. I called a place, asked about the names and the date and waited. Nothing. It was always nothing. But I still had a long way to go.

Frank always had different identities for each of us, passports, driver's licenses, debit and credit cards. He kept three of them in rotation, with a couple in reserve. He fabricated some of the documents, forged others, and stole a few too. "Identity theft is too easy," he said. "And it's only temporary." You could only use a stolen identity for a short while, hours at most, usually. Things were better with the fakes. Frank had bank accounts on a few of the more permanent identities, creating an elaborate (and maybe unnecessary) online shell game. We paid bills, kept the accounts clean and up-to-date. "No red flags," Frank liked to say. "No problems, no questions."

I memorized the important stuff, credit card numbers, phone numbers, dates of birth, addresses, anything I might need to recite on the spot, but other than that, I didn't think about the fakes Frank created, but he liked to create profiles and personalities for all of his alternate identities. Jacob Maris was a landscaper outside of Tallahassee. Gilbert Lesko was a systems analyst in Jersey City. Arthur Dodge was born in Missouri but moved around a lot before settling near Rockford, where he worked for a phone company. Frank knew the streets they lived on, the cars they drove, the clothes they wore, the books they read, the movies they watched, the music they liked, the food they ate, everything about them. "They all lead uninteresting lives," I joked with him. "That's the point," Frank said. "They have enough detail to make them unique, realistic, but nothing anyone would be interested in. Nothing anyone's going to ask about, nothing memorable enough to stick out later."

Frank had complete backstories for all of his identities, and he would joke about it, knowing that he had taken it all to its absurd end. "Arthur never wears Nikes," he told me one day when I was packing. Or, "Gilbert has Starwood points, remember," when I was making hotel reservations. "Jacob has a shellfish allergy," he reminded me when I was ordering Chinese takeout on a job (more than once). I could never remember who I was with, I joked with Frank. Me, always me, he would say.

He could have made a fortune in identity theft, would have been an effective spy or intelligence asset, something that would have taken advantage of his skills. None of that interested him, however. He wanted a simple life, he said. No life is simple, though. No matter how hard you try.

It was simple enough for Frank; he changed himself as he needed. He liked to talk about it in treatment. "Change is easy," he would say. "Think about all the changes you've already made, the different people you've been in your life, think about the person you were before you started using, think about the person you were when you were using – the person you were with your friends, your family, your boss, your sponsor, whoever. You were lots of different people, changing from one to the other depending on who you were with and how you needed to act. Sometimes you changed from one person to another in a matter of seconds. I bet I was ten different people on any given day," Frank said. "I was one person around my dad, another around my mom, another one with my sister, a different one around my friends who didn't know I was an addict, and another one around the ones who did, and on and on. I changed so easily and quickly, no one seemed to know. I thought so anyway. You've already changed. Just being here. Change is easy. Don't be trapped by who you think you were, or even who you are now. We're all going to change."

It was the only time I remember Frank mentioning his family. And I didn't ask about it. Maybe it was my invitation and I missed it. I forgot all about it.

Now here I was talking with Casey, telling her that I wasn't getting anywhere with the hotels and credit cards. I didn't tell her that her brother had more than one identity. She asked a lot of the same questions I had, and we wound up about the same place. Then she said something I hadn't thought about.

"Maybe he wasn't in a hotel."

"That's what Froehmer said, I'm sure of it," I said. "Maybe Froehmer doesn't know, not for sure. Maybe somebody told him wrong."

Where does that leave me?

"I think I can help," Casey said. I was relieved and worried at the same time. I hadn't been honest with her about a lot of things, about me and about her brother. There's a lot she could find out about us, a lot I didn't want her to know.

"I can do this," I said. "I need to."

"I know," she said. "I won't be in the way. I'll stay out of it."

I didn't want that either, not exactly.

IIIII

"I just called for a reality check," Casey said.

"You might have the wrong person," I joked.

"I'm getting inundated with calls and texts and posts and all that about Frank, about what a great guy he was. They're trying to make him out like some kind of saint. That's not who he was, you know that."

"He was no saint," I said.

"I know he was trying to be a good person," Casey said. "I know he was trying. But he left a lot of hurt too. You know that."

"He didn't look back much," I told her. "He talked about his past at the center sometimes, when it was helpful, but he didn't dwell on it. I didn't know that person."

"You wouldn't have liked him," Casey said. "That's the brother I knew the best, and I just need to vent about it for a minute."

I let her vent.

"He stole a lot back then. Stole from my parents, stole from me, and it all went up his nose or in his arm. He's high in most of my memories, birthdays, prom; he was a mess at my high school graduation. He and my father got into a huge fight. He told Frank not to go. I was crying, angry at the both of them. My father wouldn't allow Frank in the car. They were yelling at each other in the driveway. More crying. So we left him at home, and of course he drove himself. I don't know how he could drive and not wreck, but there he was, standing in the back. I saw him when I walked across the stage to get my diploma. And then he was gone. Gone for a few days. He'd taken some of my father's things, golf clubs, tools, I don't know what all. He even took some of my jewelry. He stole from me on my graduation. Took some of the gifts, envelopes of money, that sort of thing. Took it all and we didn't see him for a week or so. My father threw him out of the house when he got back."

"He never mentioned it," I told her. "He never mentioned your parents to me, maybe one time. I'm sure he was ashamed of it. He tried to be better than he was, and he was, that's all you can do."

"I know," Casey said. "I'm proud of him for that, believe me. I know that he was better with you, better with everyone. It doesn't take away the hurt though. And the way he died, well, it brings it all back. I know he wasn't that person anymore, but he's not who they say he is now, either. Does that make sense?"

"Give me their names," I said. "I'll tell them to only to say bad things to you about Frank." At least she laughed.

"That's all I needed," she said. "I knew you'd understand. I knew you'd be honest with me. I can't talk to anyone else about it."

"Neither can I," I said. "I can't hardly talk about it at all."

20 THE END

I DIDN'T KNOW HOW TO CONTINUE. There was nothing left to follow, nothing I could see anyway. I didn't know what to do. Frank had it figured right; there are forces at work in our lives we can't control. Everybody gets caught in the end; everything ends in tragedy, one way or another. No one can avoid it. Maybe you can't even avoid the guilt. That's what weighed heaviest on me at times. I had gotten Frank into all of this. Maybe he would have beat the system if not for me, maybe he would have never wound up somewhere stuck in the arm for the last time. Frank could have had a good life if not for me. Frank could have outsmarted everyone; it was right there in front of him the whole time, every single day. It was my life that was the force Frank couldn't overcome. But he did. He got out. That's how you beat them. But how do you continue after that? What more is there to say?

IIIII

It wasn't as if half my life had been taken away; all of it was gone. Frank's life and my life had become so intertwined that there was no way to separate them. If he was gone, I was gone too. I had lost everything and I didn't know what to do. I didn't know how to eat, sleep, wake, walk, read, think, move, anything. I couldn't get into the bed. I could still smell him in the sheets, even after I washed them three or four times. I would put the sheets and pillow cases back on but I couldn't lie down in them. If I had somewhere else to go, I would have gone, but I didn't have the time to find a new place. So I stayed on the couch. It didn't really matter anyway; I wasn't sleeping. I sat on the couch with the TV on, the images flashing and the sound just above inaudible, all of it flickering and murmuring in the distance of the dark room. I did that for hours, for days. I did nothing, knowing I should be doing something, anything other than what I was doing, but I couldn't. I wanted to go on; I wanted to find out what exactly had happened to Frank, but I was at a loss as to how to go forward. It was all that had kept me going for a short while, then that hit a dead end. I kept thinking about a line from *The Maltese Falcon*. Sam Spade says "When a man's partner is killed, he's supposed to do something about it." I kept thinking about it, but I didn't know what to do.

IIIII

I started to go to meetings again. I wasn't going to drink or anything else – it never entered my mind, actually – I just needed some structure to the day, to see someone, people who knew Frank, some who knew me. I would wake up in the morning, go out and get a coffee, try to do some reading, and then walk about two miles to a meeting and then walk back home afterward. Sometimes the walk was the best part. There's satisfaction in repetition, consolation and comfort in the routine. You take the same path at the same time every day and you start to notice the patterns, the way the gears work, silently and efficiently, unnoticed mostly. There were the same people at the coffee shop ordering the same thing every morning, the same people at the same tables reading, the same people walking the same streets. There was the man on his way to work who never knew what coffee to order, and then always ended up getting the latte, always. There was the woman who always sat at the same table, reading her tablet and absent-mindedly chewing on her long dark hair. There was the husband and wife I always saw at the same intersection, with a baby carriage and a big black Chow, the only thing different from one day to the next was who had the carriage and who had the dog. There were mostly the same people in the group, sitting in the same chairs, saying the same things. I saw the same guy on his bicycle afterward, always smiling, always giving everyone a big thumbs-up as he rode past. It all made me feel good, or at least better. There were still things you could count on in the world.

And I still talked to Casey. She called every day. She never brought up Frank; she always let me bring him up. She talked about her day. She talked about her work.

"I've never talked to a pediatric surgeon before," I said.

"No need," she said.

I told her that I had a daughter. "No need for surgery, though."

"That's good," she said and then told me about a nine-month-old with knife wounds she had to operate on. "The mother stabbed him for crying. She couldn't hear the TV. She said it like it made absolute sense."

It's a whole different world there, I told her. For some reason I thought she lived in the same city as her parents. She did not. She lived only about an hour and a half away. Frank and I could have seen her all the time. Frank never mentioned her. I tried to be wary, but it was hard with her. She was easy to talk to, and easy just to listen. She said she lived by herself and said she was happy to be alone.

“I keep busy,” she said and then told me that she started to go to meetings too. “I learn a lot about myself, even if I don’t say anything,” she told me.

“There’s a lot of people who’ve been through what you went through, your whole life,” I said. “But sometimes you never know that until you walk into that room.”

“I don’t like all of it,” she said. “I don’t like a lot of it, but I get something out of it every time I go.”

“That’s all you need. Hang on to the stuff that helps.”

Casey had some of the same cadence as Frank in the way she talked, especially when she was excited about something. It shocked me the first time I noticed it, like hearing a piece of music you thought you’d never hear again. I didn’t like it, but then the more I heard it, the more I wanted to hear it. I never told her; I just waited for it. It always came, that echo on the other end of the phone.

Then one day she called and changed everything. “I got the police report,” she said. “Frank wasn’t found in a hotel like we thought.”

Like we were told.

“He was found on the street.”

Casey gave me the address. It wasn’t far from where we’d done the job.

“Froehmer didn’t know what he was talking about,” Casey said.

Or maybe he did. Maybe he knew exactly what he was saying. It didn’t matter in the short run; I had something to do, somewhere to start again. The confused coffee guy and the hair-eating girl and the baby/Chow couple and the group and the thumbs up biker would all have to do without me. They wouldn’t even notice. I was sure of that. I was the one gear with no teeth. Not yet anyway. They were starting to come in, though. And they were going to be sharp.

21
THE ARREST

I HAD PLANNED ON HEADING BACK TO THE CITY TO INVESTIGATE WHAT CASEY HAD TOLD ME, HAD EVEN RENTED A CAR AND WAS READY TO GO, WHEN FROEHMER CALLED. "Sit tight on that other thing for a minute," he said. He had another job. It didn't seem worth it; the smallness of it. "It's nothing," Froehmer said. "It'll get you back in it, get your mind off your troubles. You'll see. It'll be good for you. It's easy."

I went about it like any other job, except it wasn't like any other job. I had to try to think like Frank, to remember all the things he did, a lot of them I could never do, not as well as he could anyway. I sat in the car, by myself for the first time in a long time, and tried to use Frank's equipment to check the house for cameras, security, access their systems, try to take down their internet if possible. Some of it worked, I guess. I wasn't going to need any of that anyway; I was going to sit and watch and wait and get in and out and be done with it. The rest was just practice, and something to do while I sat alone for hours. It was busywork, the same as the job. Froehmer had practically said as much. I wondered if he had someone else taking over for the trophy after all. I wondered if he had someone taking over for the jobs we used to do. I wondered if I'd been demoted. Maybe I wouldn't be back on the better gigs. Maybe I didn't care. I'd have to do whatever Froehmer said, for a while anyway, a long while, until he figured I'd paid him back for his help with Frank and the funeral and all that. I was back in a hole with him and would have to work it off. It was going to take a while with jobs like this, I thought.

IIIII

I sat and watched the house and noticed a car parked about halfway down the block behind me. No one got out of it and it stayed parked for about an hour, then drove off. A few minutes later another car came and parked almost in the same spot and no one got out of it either. I was being watched.

I had taught Frank to always get out of the car when you park. Just in case someone is watching. Whoever was driving would get out and walk away, usually to the back of our target house to get a good overview (it had to be done anyway), and then, when the area seemed secure, the other one would text for him to come back to the car. Sometimes we'd both walk away, just like anyone else would after they park. You don't just sit there. Unless you want to be obvious. The guys behind me were obvious. Cops on the job, I thought. Who else would be that lazy?

I let them sit there and then I drove off. I was driving around, half-hoping they would follow me just so I could lose them, when the thought occurred to me that maybe they weren't cops. Maybe they were somehow connected with Frank. It didn't make sense, but I thought about it anyway. I turned around and went back to the house. I had wasted about a half an hour and by the time I got back to the target, the car was gone. Cops, I figured, which also didn't make much sense. Maybe it was nothing. Frank would have left, waited for another time to do the job. I had the place figured. I could be in and out in a few minutes, gone long before anyone would notice. Even if they were cops, or someone else. They weren't going to stop me. I circled around and then parked a few blocks away and walked back to the target. There was no one around.

I went inside the house and found what I needed in less than a minute. I could have done the job. I could have grabbed the stuff and been gone. But I didn't. I'd like to say that it was because of the cars on the street, the ones watching me, but I hadn't really thought about that. I thought I had shaken them. How would they even know to watch me? I hadn't even thought that much about it, to be honest. I just stood there and decided I didn't want to do the job. Not that day anyway. So I turned around and went back out. I got about halfway down the block when two guys approached me. "You're under arrest," one of them said, and they both showed me badges. I didn't say anything. They took me to their car and put me in the backseat. No one said anything as we drove to the station. I didn't have anything to worry about. I hadn't done anything.

I never carried any ID, no credit cards, nothing with a name on it, not even a fake one, whenever I went into a house. I only had some cash in my pocket. All I had to do was to keep my mouth shut. They tell you right up front to stay quiet. "Anything you say can and will be used against you." Anything. So I wasn't going to say one word.

It wasn't until we got to the station that they realized I hadn't done anything. I didn't have anything on me, not even the car keys (I left them in the glove compartment). All I had was about a hundred bucks in my pocket. They didn't care. They wanted to ask me some questions. I didn't say a word. They wanted my name. Nothing. They wanted my address. Nothing. They wanted to know what I was doing in that part of town. Nothing. They took me to a room and both cops sat me down and asked me the same questions all over again, and I gave them the same answer. I sat and didn't open my mouth.

They left and came back with another cop. He tried a different approach. "You're not in any trouble," he told me. "Not yet anyway. We just want to get some information. We had a tip and maybe it's just a case of you being in the wrong place at the right time, something like that. Maybe you could help us out here."

I thought about quoting *Bartleby, the Scrivener* but even that was too much to give them. I exercised my right and remained silent. God, does that piss them off.

"We can hold you here until we get some answers," the third cop said.

I let them try to threaten me for a while, then I spoke. Just one word, which I repeated three different times. "Lawyer." "Lawyer." "Lawyer."

They all left the room again. After sitting by myself for almost an hour they came back one last time. And let me go.

I had to take a car back to get the rental. I figured they knew who I was anyway, or at least knew the car, and the name I'd rented it under. Frank would burn that identity immediately. I would too, but it had to wait. I texted Froehmer. He'd need to know that the job was off. "Blown," I wrote. I could see he'd read it and that the message was deleted, but there was no reply. That would wait too.

|||||

I had to meet Froehmer at the diner. It was like being called to the principal's office. He'd waited a day to summon me. I figured he knew what had happened before he asked me. "No luck?" he said.

"It wasn't right," I told him. "Someone was staked out on the street."

"You saw them?"

"You couldn't miss them."

Froehmer sat back and drank his coffee.

"That's all of it?"

"I could go back," I said.

He shook his head. "You did right. Another time."

"I want to see this through. I don't want to make it a habit."

"You didn't get caught though, did you?" Froehmer said. "That's the habit I want."

"How'd they know to be there?"

"Do we even know who they were?"

"I was hoping you'd know." I didn't know what Froehmer knew and what he didn't know. He was connected to a lot of people, cops, crooks, lawyers, most everyone in town. He never let on about anything, or hardly anything, but I always assumed he knew everything and tried to work from there. But just because he knew everything, didn't mean I had to tell him all of it. I tried to only tell him enough, to see what he might say on his own. I was trying to make some sense of it. Pieces were taking shape, but I didn't know how they all fit together.

"I'm going to find out," Froehmer said. He drank some more coffee. "How are you doing otherwise?" He'd asked me that when we first sat down. I told him the same thing. "I'm doing all right."

"You need to keep busy," he repeated. "You're good on your own. You proved that."

I wondered if that was the point of it. You never knew with him. He made everything seem like a test, as if you were always auditioning for something, something you never knew was available or not. All I knew was that I didn't care if he called with another job or not. I didn't want to be busy. I didn't want to listen to Froehmer tell me what I needed and didn't need. I didn't want to hear anything. I didn't want to sit in a car without Frank. I didn't want any of it. I wanted to go back and find out what happened. That was going to keep me busy enough. But I knew Froehmer would call again. He had me under him. I couldn't walk away, no matter what I wanted.

We walked out of the diner and Froehmer started to walk away without a word. "I've got something for you," I told him, and we walked down the street to my car. Froehmer stayed on the sidewalk as I went to the passenger-side door of the car. He was cautious, I thought. I reached in and got a brown paper bag and handed it to him. Froehmer took it and looked inside. It was the object he wanted from the job. I wasn't going to take it, but once the cops let me go, I was so mad I went back and took it anyway.

Froehmer was surprised. I could see it in his face, one of the few times I'd ever seen him show it. Maybe he was impressed. "I knew you could do it," he said. "I knew you still had it. You're a smart kid."

I was trying to stay a step ahead of Froehmer, but I didn't really know what I was doing. Maybe it had been a test. Maybe I passed.

"Like I said, I don't want to get into the habit of not finishing things."

"You did all right," Froehmer said. "I know it hasn't been easy, but you're going to be okay." He nodded his head and put the bag under his arm.

"I'm ready to work," I said.

"I know you are. I'm going to ask about moving you up." He suddenly seemed startled and quickly got into his car. "I'll send someone around with something extra for you."

I went home and thought about what he said. He was going to ask about moving me up. It was the first inkling that I had of being part of an organization. I always knew that Froehmer didn't work alone, that I wasn't even the only one working for him, stealing for him, but it was the first time he'd ever mentioned it out loud. And it was the first time he gave an indication that he wasn't at the top of the organization. He reported to someone the same way I reported to him. I didn't know if I liked it. I knew I didn't like the fact that someone else probably knew all about me, someone I didn't know at all. Froehmer was going to talk to them about me. About moving me up. I didn't know if I wanted to move up. I didn't even know what it meant. I certainly didn't want him talking about me. But what could I do about it?

The more I thought about it, the more I thought that the reason that this conversation had happened now wasn't because I'd passed whatever test they had for me, it was because Frank was gone. Froehmer had never liked us together from the beginning, and maybe his boss (or bosses) didn't either. They only tolerated it because we got the work done. We could have moved up together, the two of us. We should have. It should have at least been talked about. Maybe that was the message Froehmer was sending. I was right where they wanted me. I wasn't going anywhere they didn't want me to go. Only I was.

22
THE DOORS

I WENT BACK TO THE CITY, BACK TO THE NEIGHBORHOOD WHERE WE'D DONE THE JOB, BACK TO WHERE FRANK HAD RETURNED AND NEVER COME BACK, BACK TO THE HOUSE WHERE IT ALL STARTED, BACK TO WHERE THERE HAD TO BE ANSWERS.

I didn't know how else to go about it, so I started knocking on doors. When they answered I had a pad and pen in my hand and I said, "I'd like to ask you about the murder that took place in the neighborhood." That always got their attention. Most of them didn't know anything about it. Most of them didn't know anything at all. They wanted their own answers. Most of them never knew there was a body found down the block. They thought they were safe. They wanted to know why they weren't.

I never said I was the police, or anything. I never had to say I was anything. All I said was that I was investigating a murder that had happened in the neighborhood. Maybe people assumed I was a cop. I will admit that I went to a thrift store and bought an old suit, one that looked as if some detective had sat at his desk in the thing for ten years or more. I dressed the part, that's true, but I never said who I was or what I was. Maybe they thought I was a reporter because of the notebook I had. I never cared and they never asked. They all talked. That's all I cared about. But most of them had nothing to say.

During the day the street was deserted. I could have robbed almost every house on the block in about twenty minutes. Everybody worked or had better places to be during the day. There were a few nannies who watched small children. They weren't around at night, hadn't been there to see anything, and the one who was there was fast asleep. There was a woman dying across the street from the target house. She had hospice care and the caregiver answered the door. I could see the woman in the living room, propped up in a hospital bed. She was too young to be on her way out. The caregiver spoke English fine, but with a thick accent. Somewhere in Africa, I thought, and then was embarrassed by my ignorance. It was like thinking she was from somewhere in North America, or the Southern Hemisphere. What did I know about it? The caregiver didn't know anything about what I needed to know. "I'm not here at nights," she said. "Never at night. Eight to eight. That's when I'm here."

I went back to the car and looked up the addresses of the houses on the street. I looked at when they were bought and sold, who bought them and how much they paid for them. I'd only made it through a few when someone came back home down the street. I went and knocked and knocked and no one came to the door for a long time. I'd just seen them go in and now here they were ignoring the door. Finally, the man came and opened the door just far enough to get a look at me. I could see his shirt was freshly untucked and he wasn't wearing shoes.

"I'm hoping you can help me with a murder that happened down the block," I told him.

"What murder?"

"A man was murdered around the corner, or his body was found there anyway. I was wondering if you knew anything about it."

"I don't know the slightest thing about it. You tell me."

I told him when it happened and showed him a photograph of Frank. "They found him just around the corner," I told him.

The man shook his head. "I don't know anything about it. I wish I did."

That was the response of almost everyone who talked to me. I kept knocking up and down the block. A character straight out of Chandler answered the door a couple of houses down from the target house. His eyes had crawled back into his skull and weren't sure they wanted to come back out. I knew his story even before I saw the cooker and syringe on the coffee table behind him.

I hadn't expected to find that, not on this street. I stood and explained myself and he stood and sort of listened. He wouldn't know anything, not for a while, I thought.

"I don't want to bother anyone," he said.

"You might want to bother somebody," I said, looking past him. "I've been right where you are, believe me."

He took my arm and brought me inside and closed the door. "I'm thinking about quitting," he said.

I didn't know what to do. Frank did this sort of stuff but not me. "It takes about three years," I said, "sometimes five." I regretted saying it.

"I quit before. Then had some surgery and they put me back on."

"When was that?"

"I was clean for almost nine months."

"It's all part of it," I said. "Relapse is still recovery."

He nodded. "I've been told that before."

"It's still true. You want me to call someone? Take you somewhere?"

"I'll be all right," he said. "Tell me about your friend again."

"My friend died," I told him, "right down the block. He'd been sober for about ten years. Then got mixed up with somebody around here. That's where they found him anyway. Can I show you the picture again? Maybe you've seen him."

I showed him the picture. He still didn't know.

"Maybe you know someone who sold him some stuff," I said.

He didn't know.

"Maybe you can tell me who you use, maybe he knows my friend."

"No one regular," he said. He told me where he went. He bought from anyone. It didn't matter, he thought. "Ten years?" he said.

"What?"

"Ten years. Your friend."

"That's right."

I had him until then. He would have gone with me, I think; he would have gotten help. Here I went and told him it would take three, five at the most. I shouldn't have said it. You never do. It takes as long as it takes. I had to say something and I said the wrong thing. He would have gone, even then, with me saying the wrong thing, but then I had to mention Frank and the ten years.

He wasn't going anywhere now. He was done with me. I didn't know what I was talking about, just like everybody else. If I had stayed on him, I could have helped, but I had to swing things back to Frank, back to why I was there. I wasn't there for him. I could have been.

He opened the door.

"I could take you somewhere," I said.

"Where your friend went?"

"Anywhere you want."

"I could use some money for the bus," he said.

"I'll take you."

"That's okay," he said. "I've got people who can help."

He closed the door.

I knocked again but he didn't come back. I stood and waited, then went back to the car. I had to force myself to go and knock on a few more doors. No one knew anything, not even the person right next door.

"I'm having a hard time tracking down some of the people on the street," I told her. "Like next door. Do you happen to know anything about them?"

"Oh, he's never around," the neighbor said.

"He?"

"Single guy, I think. I haven't seen him in a while. Travels a lot, I think."

I asked about the wife and the kid, but she didn't think that was right.

"Lives alone as far as I know. Haven't seen him around in a while." The neighbor gave me his name. I wrote it down and thought she didn't know what she was talking about. Maybe she was confused about it. It put me in a foul mood and I went back to the car and thought about forgetting about the day and all the people I made the mistake of meeting. It was getting late, but not late enough. I thought I should wait around until after eight and talk to the caregiver at the house across the street. I went and got something to eat and wasted time until I could come back. I wasn't expecting much, but then I'd been wrong all day.

The other aide was still there; she helped explain what I wanted to know. She took charge and hardly let me speak. If there was anything to know, she was going to know it. The night aide was from Honduras. I didn't have to ask, the other aide told me. Her name was Marina. They'd been working together for almost two years now. "The agency likes how we work with each other, I guess," Marina said. I stood there and nodded my head as Marina and the other aide talked at me. "Show her the picture," the aide told me and I showed it to Marina.

"I don't know," she said. "But I saw two men come out of the house that night, around the time you're talking about."

"Do you know who he was with?" the first aide asked Marina.

"With the man who lives in the house," Marina said.

"You saw him?"

"I saw them come out of the house. They were on the sidewalk, and then walked down the street. I saw it. I was right at the window."

"You saw this."

"I was right there," Marina said, and pointed to a place on the floor, right in front of a window. "And they were right there." She pointed to the sidewalk across the street, in front of the house. "I didn't think anything about it. They just walked down the street. But I saw them. Maybe he should be arrested, the man who lives there."

"Maybe he will be," I said. "We'll need more information than what you saw, but it's a big part of what we need to know. Someone might be back to talk more to you, if that's okay."

"All I know is what I saw. It was only a couple of seconds. But sometimes that's all it takes."

Maybe the guy across the street didn't do the actual deed, but he knew who did. Perhaps he took Frank right to the guy who gave him the shot. I could have saved a lot of time and just knocked on that door across the street. It was right there.

Except I had a job to finish. I couldn't freelance around the neighborhood like some amateur detective chasing a half-baked hunch; my time was Froehmer's and I had to go and get the trophy all over again. Froehmer would hang that over me forever. Only he wouldn't tell me that directly; he had Mobley call me. "You know what to get and where," Mobley said. "Now's the time." I asked for a couple of days, thinking maybe I could get some answers by then, but Mobley wouldn't even give me that. "Get it now," he said. "Tonight." It didn't work that way, I told him, but Mobley wouldn't listen. It didn't matter what I wanted to do; the machinery had started to move and nothing could stop it.

23 THE KID

"DO YOU HAVE A GUN?" Frank said. It might have been the second time he came on the job with me. He was still trying to figure it out, seeing all the angles and wondering how I dealt with them.

"Don't want one, don't need one," I said.

"What would you do if someone walked in on you?"

"It's never happened."

"But it might. What would you do?"

I used to think about that a lot. I even thought about carrying a gun or a knife, just in case. But it wasn't worth it. Besides, it was correcting a problem at the end, instead of taking care of it before it ever happened. You eliminated that chance, or reduced it as much as possible. I used to think about it, but now I never did.

“Run, I guess. If I could,” I said.

“What if they have a gun?”

“I’d get shot then, or arrested.”

“They might kill you,” Frank said.

“They might. If I fuck up bad enough. But I’d rather be killed for my own mistake than kill someone else. Getting arrested for B and E is a whole lot different than getting arrested for murder. But it’s not going to happen.”

“This is how it works,” Frank said. “Wherever somebody’s got more than somebody else, there’s stealing, and wherever there’s stealing, there’s going to be killing.”

“Not by us,” I said.

“Let’s get out before it comes to that,” Frank said. “Because it will come.”

IIIII

I sat and watched the house for a few hours, watched them all leave the way they did every morning, first the father, then the son, then the mother. They were all out the door and gone before a quarter past eight. I sat and waited anyway. I almost drove off. I wasn’t sure I wanted to go in and get the trophy, wasn’t so sure I wanted to undo what Frank had done. He’d put it back, why should I go and take it. It was like I was stealing from him. I tried to put that thought out of my mind. That would get me nowhere. I had to do it for Frank, to correct what we’d done wrong, to finish what we’d been hired to do. That’s all there was to it. I could be in and out in less than five minutes. Less than three, I bet. But I sat and thought about it. I could have done it twenty times for all the time I sat and thought. Superstition had gotten the better of Frank; I couldn’t let it get the better of me.

IIIII

Finally, I had the trophy in my hand and was good to go, but stopped and looked around the room. There was a framed photo on the wall I hadn’t noticed before, a grainy, yellowed image of athletes shaking hands after a game, guys in shorts and jerseys, some with helmets still on. It was an old newspaper clipping, with the caption cut off. I studied the faces, thinking one of them looked familiar. It was a faded face in the background, partially obscured by other faces, but I kept coming back to it. He looked like someone I knew. It was impossible to tell, but I thought he looked like Froehmer. I looked at the face until it became nothing but disconnected dots. Maybe it was a young Froehmer, maybe not. It was impossible to tell. There was no date on the photo, not even an indication what paper it came from. I didn't even notice the team names on the jerseys. That never occurred to me, I guess. I was looking only at the faces, and then I forgot about it. I had other things to think about.

I was starting down the stairs, when the kid appeared in the hallway. He let out a "Hey!" or just a yelp of surprise that almost made me drop my bag. He charged up the stairs toward me and I backed up to the landing. He came up fast, not thinking, probably had no idea what he was going to do when he got to me. But I knew. When he got close enough, I kicked him right in the crotch. He bent forward and fell backwards in an awkward way that would have seemed funny on its own, the kind of shit people laugh at on TV or online. But he was at the bottom of the stairs and not moving. He'd hit his head a couple of times on the way down, and I was afraid he'd broken his neck or something. I watched him and waited for him to get up, or even move, but he didn't. I hurried down the stairs and put my hands close to his nose and mouth. He was still breathing. I could see his eyelids starting to flutter. He was going to come to and I rushed out of the house and got in the car and drove home. Somewhere along the way, I decided that I would not give the trophy to Froehmer, not right away, anyway. It had all gotten fucked up and I thought I might need it. I needed something. And then things got a lot worse than just fucked up.

24
THE MACHINE

I WAS NEVER SOMEONE I LIKED, NOT FOR A LONG TIME, NOT NOW. I made too many mistakes. I didn't have time enough to figure out who I was or what I wanted. I was a father before I was a man, not sure what I was doing or what I could do. Then I had to go to work, do what my father said, what Froehmer said. If I had known earlier, maybe things would have been different, but then I never would have met Frank. You can make a lot of mistakes and still wind up all right. For a while anyway. I walk through the world with my faults alone. I'm not making excuses. I know who I am and what I've done. I don't recognize any judgment over me but I know all the same that I will be judged. This is less a confession than a declaration, I suppose, not even an explanation really. I'm not trying to justify myself, but a chance to tell my story, before it gets told for me. I wonder if I'm where I am because of who I was, the son of a crook. Maybe I had no chance, not from the beginning, since that's when my father, and Froehmer, started on me. It had already begun, long before I came along, and I got caught up in a machine that had already been running, had already figured out what to do with someone like me. I'm not blaming anyone, but maybe it wasn't all me; maybe it was my father and then Froehmer who made me the way they wanted, acted on me and shaped me, programmed me exactly the way they wanted. They wanted me to think I was making my own decisions, but I was always going to be working for Froehmer. It's a dodge to say it's not my fault, but it's a lie to say I wasn't going to wind up like this one way or the other.

25 THE PINCH

"DID YOU HEAR ABOUT THE MURDER?" Casey asked.

"No," I said.

"Somebody killed a kid, right around the corner from where Frank was found."

"What? When was that?" My mind was racing. Maybe he wasn't all right when I left him. Maybe was hurt a lot worse than I thought and now he was dead and I'd killed him.

"Just the other night," she said. "Somebody shot him. Just around the corner from where Frank was killed. You think they're connected?"

Shot him. What was that about? It was worse than me killing him, I thought. Now it meant that somebody had gone into the house after I had and murdered the kid.

“Where did you hear all this?”

“It was on the news,” Casey said. “You didn’t know about it?”

“No. I don’t know anything.”

“But you think they might be connected? The kid and Frank?”

“I don’t see how they couldn’t be.” I had half a mind to hang up on her and head for another country. I wasn’t sure why I was hanging around now anyway. It was one thing to get picked up for breaking and entering, now they’d be trying to pin a murder on me.

“Right?” Casey said. “I wonder what it means. The kid didn’t even live there, the news said. It was just some family staying there.”

“Just staying there? What do you mean?”

“They didn’t live there, I guess. The husband was there for work. It was an Airbnb thing, or something, just for a few months. And here somebody broke in and tortured the kid before killing him. You think that’s what they did to Frank?”

“No,” I said. “It doesn’t sound the same at all. Maybe they’re not related. You think that’s possible?”

“I don’t know. They don’t even mention Frank on the news. I feel like I should call them.”

“I wouldn’t do that,” I said. “The cops aren’t going to tell the news all they know. They have their reasons for what information they put out. I’m sure they’re working on it.”

I could get out, if I got out right then, I thought. But where would I go? If I went, I was gone, gone forever. If I stayed, well, I knew what was going to happen. I would have to play it out. The cops would come. I’d get arrested. Maybe there’d be a trial. I couldn’t see how that would go against me, but you never know. Here I thought I’d been so clever, and I acted like a dumbshit. Now there’d be cops and questions, and probably a death on my hands. And I didn’t care. I didn’t care about the kid. I didn’t care that he was dead, not really. I only cared that I could get saddled with it. And I didn’t really care about that, except that none of it got me any closer to who had done that to Frank. That was reason enough to stick around. I'm not saying it was a good reason, but it was the only thing I had at the moment.

IIIII

A few days later I was out getting a coffee, early, with hardly anyone on the street yet. I walked around a while, took my time, trying to focus my thoughts. By the time I got to the coffee place, there was a line. I didn't want to be around people, but there I was standing inches away from fifteen or so bodies.

I could smell the kid, see his face, his eyes closed there at the bottom of the stairs. Maybe they'd shot him right there, but they hadn't. They slapped him around and then shot him. The same guy (or plural) who had gone after the kid would be after me, I thought. But what could the kid tell them? He didn't know anything. That's why they'd slapped him around, and worse. I could see him there, could feel his breath on the back of my hand, could see his eyes moving under the thin skin of the lids.

I had to focus on the sound of the coffee maker, the pound of the filter as the old grounds got knocked out, the hiss of the steamer, the names called out to come get their cup. I tried to think about what name I would use, and when it came time, I forget what I had decided and said, "Frank," without even thinking. It bothered me.

I stepped outside and walked down the block. Mobley came out of nowhere and stopped me.

"Do you have it?" he said.

I shook my head.

"You're in a pinch," he said. "I'm here to make sure you don't make things worse."

He made a call on his phone and handed it to me.

"What did you do?" Froehmer said.

"I didn't do anything."

"A kid? You don't know what you've done."

"I didn't do that," I said. "I don't have a gun. You know that."

"If they find out . . . They won't need a gun to pin this on you if they find out you were in there."

"I was careful," I told him.

"But you didn't get the thing."

"Somebody beat me to it. Whoever got the kid got the thing. And it wasn't me."

It was a long enough pause that I thought maybe he was gone. He wasn't.

"Were you down there nosing around?"

"I talked to some neighbors," I said. "I wanted to find out about Frank."

"I told you to leave that to me. If you'd taken care of business first you wouldn't be in this mess. A lot of people can put you there. You know what that means?"

I knew.

"They saw the guy come out of the house, with Frank."

"They got it wrong. Way wrong. They didn't have anything to do with this. And now a kid's killed. You know what that means?" I knew.

"What were you telling these people, knocking on all these doors? Did you tell them who you were? Did you tell them you were a cop?"

"I didn't say anything. I never said that. I didn't say anything."

"They're going to come and find you," Froehmer said. I didn't know if he meant the people responsible for the kid, or the cops. It didn't matter.

"I'm fine with that," I said.

"I'm not fine with it."

"There's nothing to worry about. Nothing for you to worry about."

"We'll see," Froehmer said. "For now, we've got to get some distance. Mobley will tell you what to do. Listen to him. It'll help, but I don't know how much. There's only so much we can do. The rest is on you, understand. Listen to Mobley."

Mobley told me to get over to a warehouse and do whatever needed to be done. He told me that I'd been working there for four weeks. He handed me some old pay stubs. He said they had timecards to show I'd been working at the time the kid was killed.

"Froehmer's done his part," Mobley said, "now all you've got to do is yours."

Froehmer had it all figured out. I was sure the cops would know everything too. I had fucked up, really fucked up. But then knowing something and proving it are two entirely different things. That was the only play I had. But Mobley wasn't done.

"But this is it," he said, and I didn't know if he was talking on behalf of Froehmer or for himself. "You screw this up and you're on your own."

He still wasn't done. "If you know about the thing you were supposed to deliver, you should let us know. If you know where it is. You should produce the thing, like you were supposed to, if you can."

"You know as much as I do about it," I said. "Probably more."

I wondered if Mobley was above me or below me in Froehmer's organization. He didn't do anything more than whatever Froehmer told him to do, nothing that required any thinking on his own. He did what he was told. Maybe that placed him ahead of me. When he spoke, he spoke for Froehmer, that definitely put him ahead of me, but he couldn't be trusted on his own, not the way I was. Or so I thought. But I could do what I was told too. So I reported to the warehouse and they put me to work.

I had to drive thirty-plus minutes outside of town to get to the bland beige building that took up plenty of acres that could have been put to better use. It took me almost as long to find out where I needed to go as it did to drive there. I went from one person to the next, sitting in one chair or another while they went off and shuffled this paper or that. I sat there and hoped I wouldn't be do any of that. No paper pushing for me. I shouldn't have hoped. It was worse. I wasn't pushing paper in the office; I was pushing the paper the office threw out. I was a garbage man. For the whole warehouse. I collected all the trash that the maintenance crews collected and hauled it to a central location. It wasn't just the trash from the office, it was also trash from the warehouse. It wasn't a warehouse that stored things to be shipped out; it was a warehouse where they stored the shit people sent back. Boxes and boxes, by the truckloads, came in all day all the time. People sent back perfectly good things, but also broken things, damaged things, stuff that looked twenty years old, and all kinds of crap, books, games, clothes, appliances, food, plants, you name it, somebody had bought it then turned around and sent it back. People also sent back other stuff, dead things, dead animals, rotten vegetables, boxes of shit, literal shit. Some guy sent back boxes of dirt, at least fifty boxes of dirt. They sent back things that had oil, or worse, poured on them. "Most people don't respect property," Frank had said more than once. "Thieves respect property," I joked. "Maybe more than anyone else. They respect it so much that they want it for themselves so they can better, perfectly respect it."

"But we don't keep it," Frank said.

"I guess we respect it so much, we want someone else to appreciate it as much as we do."

And now here I was seeing all that disrespect, all that stuff that had to be sorted through and thrown out. There were loads of it, mounds of it, truck after truck of it; it never seemed to stop, as if there was a machine somewhere in that enormous building that was pumping it out faster than I could carry it off. It was shit work, but what was I going to do about it? I kept my mouth shut and did what they told me, hour after hour, and tried not to think about anything else except what was in front of me. I wore a dumb orange helmet and orange vest for safety, and drove around on my own forklift and something they called a burden carrier, which could not have been more on the nose. I would drive around on my burden carrier and imagine that I was Butch Cassidy in Bolivia, trying to go straight. I tried to imagine bandits hiding in the packed shelves, but it only depressed me to know that no one was waiting. In fact, hardly anyone was in the warehouse at all. There were rows and rows of crap, miles and miles of boxes and bins, crates and containers, stacks and stacks of it moving around on its own, controlled by algorithms and automation. There were robotic arms waiting at stations, and the stacks would make their way to them. Every now and then I'd pass by the sorting station, where they opened the boxes and separated out the reusable stuff from the garbage. It was depressing seeing the other people, expressionless as they tried to move as fast as possible, trying to keep up with the machines, working for the robots it seemed.

"They haven't invented anything that can work as well as the human hand," Casey said. "When they do that, it's game over for all of us." Casey used her hands to save babies; I used mine to pick up trash.

I spent my day surrounded by bland bins and boxes, and I didn't even care to know what was in them all. I drove around all day long, mostly routine, driving around the perimeter of the building, picking up bags – clear for paper, blue for plastic and glass, and black for garbage – and cardboard boxes and whatever else found its way to the designated stations where the crap was put, but every once in a while they'd send me a text and tell me I was needed somewhere else. Usually something had been spilled and I'd have to put on some protective boots and gloves and shit and clean it up. I didn't know what it was, but it was something no one else wanted to deal with. I could have asked, but I didn't. Maybe that's what had happened to the last guy, one too many cleanups. I didn't ask. I did what I was told until it was time to go home. It was an act I had to do every day. I couldn't be myself. I couldn't be myself around anyone.

No one knew me, really knew me. Except Froehmer. He knew everything and too much. I had to keep my mouth shut. I had to be somebody else every day. I wasn't sure I could do it.

IIIII

I was exhausted all the time. More mentally than physically. I tried to jump-start my brain; I found a copy of Karl Marx's writings among Frank's books. I tried to read it at night, but I couldn't last more than a few pages at a time. Instead of a jump-start, it was more like a short-circuit. I would fall asleep sitting up, with the book in my hands. "Marx might have been wrong about communism," Frank had said, "but he was right about capitalism." It steals from the workers, steals the time a person needs for "growth, development, and healthy maintenance of the body." Workers are nothing but fuel for the fire, the grease for the wheels of the machinery. I had always avoided it, and now I was stuck inside the machine and miserable, more miserable than I could remember.

"It's designed to make you miserable," Frank had said. "Capitalism only works if everyone's unhappy. And they think they have to buy their way to happiness. It's a fool's pursuit, but that's the way it's supposed to work. The only way it can work. Everybody has to chase after something, and then be dissatisfied once they've got it and go chase after something else. We're trapped by the pursuit of happiness, but it would all come crashing down if we all were actually happy."

"Are you happy?" I said.

Frank looked up from his work, his phone and devices he was using to monitor the house from his spot in the back seat. I could see his face in the rearview mirror, that face where it seemed like all worries went to be forgotten. "I'm as happy as I've ever been," he said. "I wouldn't want anything else. I'm not chasing after anything. I've got everything I need."

He was dead two weeks later.

IIIII

I worked at the warehouse, worked and waited. I got up every morning and drove out of town and went to work, drove home at the end of the day and ate and watched TV and went to bed and got up and did the same thing the next day. I was always tired, tired when I woke up, tired when I worked, tired when I went to bed.

"You're not tired," Casey said, "you're depressed."

Maybe she was right. I talked to her almost every night. She was about the only person I talked with. I saw other people in the warehouse, but always at a distance. I was too busy driving around the huge place, picking up trash, cleaning up mess. I had a strict schedule. Everyone else did too. We were all small, silent cogs in an enormous machine. No one was paying us to talk, or to think. I wasn't cut out for this life, I thought. I thought it all the time.

"It's in your blood," Frank had told me. "It's in all of us. Or most of us. Us Americans anyway."

"We're all crooks," I said. "Because we're capitalists."

We were back in the car, which smelled like Chinese food. We'd been there most of the night. We were working. This was early on in our work together, our life together. There was more joking and teasing, to pass the time. We were getting comfortable together.

Frank laughed. "I guess that's one way to look at it, but I was thinking farther back. You know England used to ship thieves over here as punishment."

"I thought that was Australia."

"They don't hide their history as well as we do. Starting in 1718, England began shipping convicted criminals over to the colonies. About fifty thousand of them, or about twenty-five percent of the population."

"My blood doesn't go back that far," I said.

"It doesn't matter," Frank said, about as serious about it all as I'd been. He picked at his container of Chinese food and glanced at one of his screens as we waited and watched a house. "You can't dump that many thieves in one small place and not have an effect. Look what happened. They stole land, then they stole people to work on the land. It was all baked in from the beginning, from before the beginning. Maybe it's not in our blood," he said. "Maybe it's deeper than that. It's in our culture, our identity. We wouldn't be Americans without it. Everybody steals. We have to steal."

"I can stop any time I want," I said.

"Spoken like a true addict," Frank said and handed me a fortune cookie.

IIIII

I couldn't go to meetings any more during the week, and I didn't feel like it on the weekends, but once in a while I'd go, just to have someone else to talk to, someplace else to go. It depressed the shit out me, a reminder of a life I had, one that was getting further and further away. I didn't mention any of this at the meetings. Everyone thought I was doing great, steady work, structured days, sticking with the program. What could be better? "It has to help with the loss," someone said, "keeping your mind on work and all that." They'd obviously never lost someone, not like I had, not that close. They didn't know what they were talking about. "It helps," I said. "I've got a lot of support at work, everywhere, really." Every time I left a meeting I told myself I'd never go back. And then I went back. I could get addicted to my own misery, I suppose; plenty of people do. Other times I told myself that all I had to do was endure. Another month, another week; I could do whatever had to be done. All I had to do was the work.

I got a paystub every two weeks. I got the stub, but not the pay. They handed me an envelope with some cash in it, a lot less than the amount on the stub, barely enough to live on, not enough to cover my costs. This was a message from Froehmer. I couldn't listen to it much longer. I had to go talk to him. But I couldn't, not until the cops came. If I could handle them, Froehmer would get me out of the shit patrol at the warehouse. He'd never said it, Mobley had never said it, but I knew that was the deal. I never wanted the cops to come, but I couldn't wait much longer for them not to. That's the place I'd gotten myself.

It took them long enough. More than a few paystubs. I got a call at the warehouse that I was wanted in the office. There were two uniforms waiting for me. They love to come to your work, to show everyone that you're no good before they even decided if you are or not. They were standing around with their guns and batons and handcuffs and all the other harm they carry on their belts, standing around talking to everyone in the office as if they were friends. At least I knew enough to take off my toy hat and vest.

They took me into a small conference room and we all sat down and had a nice chat. They asked me about my work, how long I'd been there, what I did before that, and before that. They asked me about Frank and rehab and being clean and everything that surrounded what they wanted to ask me. They asked me if I'd been in the neighborhood where Frank was found. I gave them the truth. "A couple of times," I told them.

"What were you doing there?"

"I wanted to see the place where he died," I told them.

"Did you talk to anyone?"

"I talked to some of the neighbors."

"What did you talk about?"

"I asked them if they'd ever seen Frank there. I showed them a picture of him."

"And had they?"

"A couple of people. They saw him on the night he was killed," I said.

They paused for a second and looked at their notes. "Who saw him?"

"I don't know," I said. "A couple of neighbors. They saw him on the street, I guess, the sidewalk. Or they thought they did. I didn't write down their names or anything."

"When you were talking with the neighbors, did you ever identify yourself as a police officer?"

"Never."

"Ever identify yourself as an official, or having any position you don't have?"

"Never."

"So, how did you approach these people?"

"I just asked them if I could talk to them about a murder in the neighborhood."

"Murder?"

"Yeah. Frank's murder. Everyone was interested."

"Okay. Why were you down there?"

"I'd been told that Frank had been found in a hotel room, someone else told me that he'd been found somewhere else. I wanted to find out for myself. So I went down and talked to the neighbors."

"Who told you?"

"Frank's sister told me that he'd been found in that neighborhood. She said she'd seen the police report. We thought he'd overdosed in a hotel room. It made more sense this way. That he was killed and left there."

"Did she know you went and talked with the neighbors?"

"I don't know. I don't think I told her. I wanted to wait until I knew something."

"And what do you know?"

"I know Frank had no business in that neighborhood, no reason to be there. It's not a spot where anyone would go for drugs. There were a lot easier places to find them, if that's what he'd wanted. I know it doesn't make sense that he was there, with his arm all shot up the way it was."

"Do you know a Robert Bowie?"

"I don't think so."

"You didn't talk to him?"

"I don't know."

"He says you talked to him."

"Okay."

"He says you talked a lot about the neighbors, asking about them."

"Probably," I said. "I asked about the people who weren't around. I asked as many questions as they would let me."

"Do you know Andrew Molina?"

"Did I talk to him too? I don't know the names of the people I talked to. I don't know these people at all. I only talked with them for a few minutes."

"Did you talk to Andrew Molina?"

"I don't know. Which house was he in?"

They showed me a picture of the house. Andrew Molina was in the house we had robbed. He was the father of the kid who'd been killed. We had finally gotten where they wanted to go.

"I didn't talk to him."

"So you talked to everyone else in the neighborhood but not this guy?"

"I don't think anyone was home when I was there," I said. "Most of the people weren't home. It was in the afternoon when I was there."

"You ever go back to that house?"

"I talked to the neighbors who were there and then I left."

"Why didn't you go back?"

"I found out enough," I told them. "I know Frank wouldn't go there on his own."

"But he was seen there, by a neighbor, you said."

"He was with someone else, they said."

"Who was that?"

"I don't know. They didn't know."

"Who saw him?"

"An older woman. She was looking out the window and saw them." I don't know why I lied. They probably knew I was lying. I should have told them about the hospice aides; they probably knew about them already. I wasn't doing myself any favors.

"She knew it was your friend."

"She said she recognized him from the photo."

"Which house was she in?"

They took out a small map of the street and I narrowed it down to a couple of houses. I just kept telling them everything that had happened. Somebody must have told them I passed myself off as a cop. They brought it up again.

"And you never said you were a police officer, attorney, detective, nothing like that?"

"Never. I never had to say who I was."

"You never said you were Frank's partner or whatever?"

"I never said anything. I just asked some questions and they answered."

"You're persuasive."

"People are happy to help," I said. "If you ask nice enough. It's their neighborhood. They want to help keep it safe."

"And you're keeping it safe?"

"I'm just trying to figure out what happened to my friend."

"I thought you had it figured out."

"The what. Not the who."

"And how are you going to figure that out?"

"That's out of my league," I said. "I was hoping you could help with that." I tried to give them a good face, the kind of face Frank could give someone and put them at ease. I don't think it worked.

"I keep looking at you," the cop said, "and I know I've seen you before. I should know who you are, at least."

IIIII

I didn't say anything. I didn't know where we stood. They still hadn't quite gotten to it, and I was wondering if they would.

"What were you doing down there with Frank?"

"Nothing special. We just hung out for a couple of days."

"Where did you stay?"

"A hotel downtown; I can't remember the name. Frank took care of it."

"He booked it and paid for it?"

"I think so," I said. "It might have been a gift from someone. Every once in a while someone would do that for Frank."

"A gift?"

"Yeah, sometimes someone from the center or somewhere would give Frank something to thank him for helping them out."

"You think that's what this was?"

"I can't remember. I can try to find out."

"Maybe the name of the hotel. Let's start there."

"Sure," I said. Maybe they already knew the name of the hotel. I don't know how, we hadn't used our real names. Maybe they didn't know.

"Were you and Frank together all the time on your trip?"

"Yes," I said. "Actually, no."

"No. You weren't together."

"He went off on his own for a while," I said.

"Where did he go?"

"I don't know."

"Why's that?"

"We had a fight," I told them. "He stormed off for a while, and when he came back I didn't ask him where he'd been."

"Did this happen a lot? Him leaving you like that?"

"Never."

"What was the fight about?"

"I don't remember. Nothing important. Not important enough to remember anyway."

"He never did this before, you said, but when he did, you don't remember why?"

"Frank had his superstitions," I said, telling a truth that was a lie. "We had a fight about a horse in the street. He thought it was a sign to get out of there. We didn't know about the horse, that it wasn't dead, you know. We'd paid for the room so I wanted to stay, but he wanted to leave. So he left."

"So you had a fight and he left. What did you do during the time he was gone?"

"I went and had some coffee, I think. Maybe just wandered around. Nothing remarkable. Waited for Frank to show back up."

"How long was he gone?"

"An hour or two, maybe."

"And where did you see him again?"

"Back at the hotel, I think. We went out for dinner then. Or maybe we had room service. One or the other."

"And how did he seem when he came back?"

"Fine. I'm not sure what you're asking."

"He hadn't gone to get drugs or anything?"

"No. I would remember that. He was fine. Everything was back to normal."

"And how did you get to the city on that trip."

"I drove. The same as last time."

"You drove your car?"

"That's right."

They stood up as if to leave and I stood up too.

"Anything else you can remember, anything else that might be helpful?" they wanted to know.

"I don't think so."

"You been back to the city since that trip?"

"I don't think so," I said.

"But maybe."

"No," I said. "I haven't been back."

"Not for any reason?"

"I don't believe I have."

"Okay, I think that's all we have for now," one of them said.

"How'd you get down to the city?" the other said, almost talking over his partner.

"I have a car."

"What make?"

I told him.

"You ever drive a rental?"

"Not in a while," I said. "I have my own car."

"When was the list time you rented one?"

"I don't know. A long time ago, I guess. More than a few years. At least five years, I bet."

"Why did you rent then?"

"My car was probably in the shop."

"And you took it to the city?"

"I don't know. I could probably find out, if you need to know."

"We'll see," the cop said and they left. On that note.

What did they know about cars? That was going to stay with me. That's the way they want it. They want you to think they know more than they do. But they had to know something. You wouldn't just ask somebody about renting a car. They had a few pieces, but could they put them together? They knew something. But let them try to prove it, I thought. I knew what to do when the time would come. People in power have proven how to act – from priests to Supreme Court justices to presidents – deny, deny, deny. Even after they have them dead to rights. But they didn't have it, not yet anyway. If they got to the robbery before the murder, I was done. They wouldn't even think about looking any farther. I was as guilty as if I'd done it. Which had me thinking. I walked back through the office and didn't talk to anyone. I put on my plastic hat and orange vest and went back to work and tried not to think about it anymore.

IIIII

I told Casey about the cops. She wanted to know why they had to show up at work, why they had to talk to me in person. "Couldn't they just talk to you on the phone?"

"Maybe they think I'm the murderer," I said.

"I hadn't thought about that. Is that what you think? Seriously?"

"They're just following up. Makes sense. I was down there snooping around. We should be glad they came. I told them all about it. Maybe it will help."

"Maybe. I bet they're focused on the other, though. They have to solve that one first. Frank got knocked down by a teenager. Isn't that awful to think like that?"

"That's how it works."

"You think they think they're connected?"

"I don't think so. They didn't even say anything about the kid."

"That's why they're still in uniform," Casey said. "They won't make detective thinking like that."

There's that old joke about the two guys running from a bear and the one guy says to the other, "You think you can outrun a bear?" and the other says, "I don't have to outrun the bear, I only have to outrun you." That's how I felt. I didn't have to be smart, I only had to be smarter than the cops.

IIIII

I thought Froehmer might reach out to me after the cops had left me alone for a while, but he didn't. I was going to have to go to him. I waited until my meager savings were about tapped out and then went to him, hoping he'd bring me back to doing what I did before. "I could use some better-paying work," I told him. "I'll see," he said and left me hanging for another week. When my paystub came on Friday, it was the same as it always was, but the envelope was heavier. I wouldn't be leaving the warehouse any time soon.

26
THE TRUTH (SORT OF)

"DID YOU KNOW FRANK WAS IN A CAR WRECK THE DAY HE DIED?" Casey asked me.

Did I know? I mean, what version was I supposed to know with Casey? I couldn't remember what I'd told her or not. I couldn't keep it straight anymore. "Yeah. A little fender bender."

"Do you know where it was?"

"No," I said. "He didn't tell me." I wondered how she knew.

"It was close to where he died," Casey said. "You didn't know that?"

"No," I said. "Who told you this?"

"The police," she said, and I was worried what else they told her.

"What did they say about it?"

"That he was in an accident out there, in a rental car. Some guy ran into him, I guess. But it wasn't far from where he went back to later. Don't you think that means something?"

"Absolutely."

"Maybe he'd gone and got some drugs, got into the fender bender, then went back later and overdosed," Casey said. "Don't you think?"

"Maybe," I said. "But I don't think so."

"That's what the cops think happened."

That's what the cops were telling her. I wasn't so sure that's what they thought. I wondered if they'd told her the name on the rental. I didn't have to wonder long.

"The police said Frank was in a rental. I thought you had your car down there."

"No, we took the rental," I said.

"Who rented it?"

"We did it. But we used a different name. Did the cops tell you that?"

"They did not."

"Well we did. We used the same name for the hotel. We didn't want anyone to find us."

"You do that a lot?"

"No. Not a lot. A few times. Frank liked it. He liked pretending we were other people, especially when we went somewhere. What else did the cops say about it?"

"They said some kid ran a stop sign and hit Frank. He had to take the rental back and didn't get another one. He took a car back to the hotel. They were trying to get in touch with the kid that hit him. I guess they haven't heard from him. Jerry Caldwell. I got his contacts from the rental place."

"LA address?"

"That's right."

"Born in Singapore?"

"What do you know about him?" Casey asked.

"I know he doesn't exist," I said.

Frank didn't kill himself. I was sure of it now. I knew it just by the name of the guy who hit him. I knew all about Jerry Caldwell. It was an identity Frank had invented for Froehmer to use. Froehmer had asked me if Frank would do it; he never explained what for. He had a bank account, credit cards, a driver's license, maybe even a passport. Frank made a few of them for Froehmer, but I remembered Jerry Caldwell, because Frank was happy with that one. He thought it was clever, a name he took from someplace else (and didn't tell me). Every time Froehmer used the name Jerry Caldwell, Frank got a kick out of it. It was a joke he had over Froehmer. Only Froehmer had passed the joke on to somebody else.

IIIII

I tried to remember if I'd seen the kid who'd been driving. I must not have. I couldn't see his face. He was slumped over in the wheel, I thought. It wouldn't have mattered. I didn't know many of the guys who worked for Froehmer. Maybe he didn't work for him at all. Maybe he only did that one thing. And that one thing was to follow us, or to hit us, on purpose. But why would he crash into us? There were easier ways to stop us, if that's what he was trying to do. I thought it was probably the former. Froehmer wanted to make sure we had done the job. And whoever he got to watch us botched their part. Did that make sense? I wasn't so sure. I couldn't talk to anyone about it. I had to figure it out on my own.

"How do you know about Jerry Caldwell?" Casey wanted to know.

"It's a fake name, like the ones Frank and I used."

"You're going to have to do better than that," Casey said.

She was right. I told her she was right and to give me a minute. She waited while I tried to figure out where to begin and how to explain it. I thought it might be the last time we talked to each other, and I wondered if that wouldn't be better, better for her, I mean. Things could only get worse for me.

"I'm going to tell you some things I shouldn't," I said. "I'm going to tell you some things that can hurt me, that maybe you won't want anything to do with me anymore, and that would hurt me. I don't want that. But it's who I am, who *I* am, not your brother. He was helping me. That's all he was doing. Everything is my fault."

She didn't say anything.

"I do small jobs for people. Mostly stealing stuff. They tell me what they want and I go and get it. That's it. I never hurt anyone. Frank never hurt anyone. All we did was steal stuff for other people. That's all we were doing down there. And some guy hits us, hits Frank, some guy who apparently was using a name Frank had made up. I don't know why or how he had the name. I don't know why he was there following us or whatever it was he was doing. Maybe he was trying to stop Frank. Maybe he was going to kill him and got into an accident. Maybe he killed him later. I don't know any of it. But I know I need to find out who it was, who it really was. And we can't let the cops know about any of it. And I need to know if they told you anything else about any of it."

"They know about you," Casey said. "Or they think they do. They suspect. They told me you stole things. They said you worked for someone else. They didn't tell me anything more than that."

"It's true," I said. "But Frank wasn't part of it. He didn't know anything about who I worked for, none of that. He was only helping me. He was trying to help me get out of it. You need to know that. All your brother did was help."

"I want to help," Casey said. "But you have to tell me what happened. All of it."

I told her, more or less. Just enough for her to help, or think she was helping. I told her that we had taken something but I didn't tell her what it was, and that the job had been where Frank was killed, that he'd been killed taking the thing back. I didn't tell her it was in the house where the kid was. I didn't tell her that.

"I don't see how it makes sense," Casey said. "How does the kid fit in?"

"I don't know," I said. "Maybe he doesn't fit. Or maybe he was trying to stop whoever wanted the thing in the first place. We left someone unhappy. They wanted something and didn't get it."

"They didn't get it from Frank?"

"I think they killed Frank after he took it back. The lady said she saw him leaving the house with somebody, the guy who lived there, she said. Besides, if they got it from Frank, then why the kid? And why not come after me?"

"Maybe they don't know about you," Casey said.

"I hadn't thought about it that way," I said. It was true. I had the trophy, but no one had come after me. There had to be a reason for that. That reason might have something to do with Froehmer. It all came back to him somehow. That's where I still needed help.

3

27
THE OBLIGATION

WHEN I GOT TO MY CAR AFTER WORK, MOBLEY WAS SITTING IN THE PASSENGER'S SEAT. I had locked it. I always locked it. You never know what someone's going to take. But there he was sitting and waiting for me. I figured Mobley wasn't smart enough to get into it by himself, that he must have had help. Whoever helped him wasn't there. Only Mobley. Sitting in my car.

"Go on and drive out of here," Mobley said. "Drive as if you're going home."

I backed out of the spot and started to drive out of the parking lot. "They probably have you on camera, breaking into my car."

"They don't have me doing anything," Mobley said.

I tried to nod as sarcastically as one can and continued to drive. After we were about a half mile away from the warehouse, Mobley started giving me directions, telling me where to turn, this way and that, until we ended up down a gravel road where another car was parked. Mobley had me pull over and park so we were nose-to-nose with the other car. I thought about running. I wondered how far I would get in the dark and where I would go and if it was even worth it. I couldn't see anyone in the car. If Froehmer, or whoever he worked for, was going to kill me, it wouldn't be Mobley who did it. We both got out and walked to the empty car and got in. Now I was in the passenger seat.

"Froehmer wants to bring you back in," Mobley said.

Okay.

"You just need to do something to clean the slate," Mobley said and when he told me exactly what that meant I didn't want to come back in.

"I'm not sure it's where I can help Froehmer the most," I said. "I'm better suited for getting him stuff."

"He doesn't see it that way," Mobley said and looked out into the dark countryside. "We underestimated you. You showed what you could do with that kid."

"I wasn't part of that. Froehmer knows."

Mobley shrugged. "He knows what you need to do. The kid can come back on us just the same. Froehmer's done more than he should have for you. That's what you don't get." He leaned toward me until I could see the anger in his face. "You and your boyfriend . . . " he started to say, then started again. "You gummed it all up going down there and talking with everybody. You might as well have a sign on your back. You need to do whatever you're told to make this right."

"I don't see how this would make it right."

Mobley shrugged again. "I'm not begging anyone. You could stay picking up trash for all I care. You won't get far with Froehmer with that though."

Everything was quiet. Everything was empty.

"I told him you'd do what needed to be done."

"I know. You're never slow sticking my neck out," I said, but he didn't take it. He kept on with what he wanted.

"And there's that unfinished job from the start. The one your partner fouled up."

"I don't get you."

"Don't play innocent; you know what we want," Mobley said and came to the point.

"You find it and I'll get it," I said.

"You were there. You didn't take it?"

"It was already gone."

"And you don't know where it is."

"If I knew, I'd have it already," I said.

"Seems to me this is still on you," Mobley said.

I didn't know how much of this was coming from Mobley and how much was coming from Froehmer. I wanted to talk directly to him, but I could see that was becoming less likely.

"This is how he wants it corrected," Mobley said. "This is how it works out." He handed me a photograph with an address written on the back. "You need to take care of this guy, the way we want, and then you'll be square. That's the way it is. The only way it's going to be."

Okay.

"Leave it in the open," Mobley said. "That's it."

"I'm not sure I know how to go about this."

"You'll figure it out," Mobley said.

Everything was empty. My car sitting in front of us, the dark fields around us, the earth and the sky were empty, no lights, no stars, just darkness. There was an emptiness in Mobley and what he said, an emptiness between us, inside me and what I thought and the words I didn't say. There was an emptiness everywhere, where I lived and where I worked. It had not been there before, but everything had been emptied out. And it all had to be filled again, one way or another.

I don't know what I said. Maybe I didn't say anything to Mobley. I took the photograph and went back to my car. He turned on his headlights and practically blinded me, two suns boring directly into me. I had to wait a minute for my eyes to adjust, and I waited until the dark blankness came back. It was the same as before, dark and empty and still. There was nothing. But at least now I could see it. I hoped that Mobley would drive out first. But he didn't. He waited for me. I drove home, occasionally glancing at the photograph in the passenger seat.

IIIII

I didn't know the first thing about doing what Froehmer wanted done. It's one thing to take something from somebody; it's different when you have to take everything. You see it all the time in movies and shit like that, but how do you know if that's how it works in real life? I suppose it was no different from anything else. Not much different from my usual jobs. You plan and prepare, and pay attention to the details. Maybe it was as simple as that. So I did what I knew how to do. After work at the warehouse I drove to the address on the back of the photograph and watched and waited. I looked at the house a long time; it didn't look as if it had any money in it, or ever would again. No one came and no one went. I waited all night. There wasn't enough coffee and Chinese food to keep me awake. In the empty silence inside and outside of the car I dozed at least twice, almost twenty minutes the second time. I had a small camera on the dash just in case, and I looked at what had been recorded when I was asleep. Nothing. I had to go to work in a few hours and had done nothing but waste a night. That was all right, I'd done that before, but not by myself in a long time. I was out of practice and it made me impatient. I waited as long as I could and then had to leave to go back to the warehouse.

I struggled to get through the day. I almost fell asleep on my stupid orange cart, careening around the aisles like a drunk driver. I had to pull over and try to get my shit together. It wasn't even lunchtime. When it was time for my break I stayed on the cart and fell asleep. More than an hour later someone shoved me awake.

"You all right," he said. I'd never seen him before. He wasn't wearing an orange vest, so I figured him for a supervisor somewhere.

I nodded. "I'll be all right."

He looked at the badge hanging around my neck, memorizing my face and name. "Who's your supervisor?" I told him. "Does he know about this?"

I shook my head. "It's never happened before. I'll make up the time. It's about thirty minutes. You can take it out of my pay."

"I'll leave that to your supervisor," he said. It went on from there. For all the time he spent standing there lecturing me about not working, neither one of us was working. I could have made up the work in the time he was taking. This is why people hate work. This is why people hate authority. I sat there and let him tell me that I could get fired. You'd think the whole organization was going to collapse because I was thirty minutes late picking up the trash. If it was that precarious of an operation, maybe the whole place should collapse. Of course that wasn't the point. So he humiliated me for a few more minutes and then allowed me to go back to my job. At least he got me awake, awake with rage for the rest of the day.

I had another night with no luck. I slept more, waking every couple of hours to look at the camera footage. It was the same as looking at a still photograph of an empty street and a quiet house. I had to leave again before anything happened. I was out of sync with whoever was in the house. Froehmer knew the deal; he could get me covered at the warehouse if he wanted. But he didn't want to. He was going to keep far away from this. I was on my own, and I wasn't in a hurry. I would wait for my day off and then stay put until something happened.

I know what Frank would have done. He would have run background on the guy, found out where he worked, what his hobbies and habits were, maybe take a look at his phone. He'd have a profile of the target in a couple of hours. Maybe he'd even put a tracking device on his car. I wasn't going to do any of that. I didn't want to know who the guy was. I didn't want to know if he was married, if he had kids, a pet goldfish, nothing. I didn't want to know anything about him, not even his name. I would sit and wait and follow him and be done with it. I couldn't think about what Frank would do in my situation, because Frank would never be in this situation.

After work I went and bought a broom and some cheap clothes at Walmart. I bought too-big shoes and some oversized coveralls, a bag of socks and a baseball cap. I bought a box of nitrile gloves and a spool of thin steel wire at a Home Depot. I put everything in the trunk, still in the bags, all of it in a large garbage bag. I went home and slept most of the night and then went over and parked near the target's house. I was too late. The car was already gone. I figured that on my day off, the first night all week I didn't watch all night and early morning, he'd be an early riser. That was all right. He'd be back, and I had the time to wait him out

The car pulled into the driveway in the early afternoon and the man from the photograph got out.

He was about Froehmer's age. He had graying hair and had on a zippered windbreaker, with shorts and sneakers. He had a basketball under one arm. He was stocky and short; he might have been an athlete once, but he didn't play basketball.

He went into the house and I didn't see him again for another four hours. He was out of his workout gear, but with the same jacket, and he got into his car and I followed him to an assisted living facility.

I waited for him to enter the building and I went into the parking lot and watched. He'd parked near a security camera on the side of the building. That camera was ancient, at least a decade old, and hadn't filmed anything in years, if ever. I ran a check on the building anyway. It was all for show.

He was inside for a couple of hours, past dinner and past the last of the day. The lot was emptying out and covered in circles of artificial light. I moved my car behind another parked car so I couldn't be seen by anyone walking from the building. When he drove home, I followed him. He went back into his house and I didn't see him again until the next morning.

Most people have patterns, many by conscious design, but most by some unconscious clock that drives them into habits they would swear they don't have. My man was inconsistent in the morning, but constant in the afternoon and evening. He probably told people he worked out every morning, and maybe he thought so himself, or maybe he did something inside the house I wasn't aware of, but some mornings (and never at the same time) he went by himself to an outdoor basketball court and shot baskets. There were two courts and four baskets, and he would move from one basket to another, shooting until he made ten baskets at each net. It took him forever. Each shot was a line drive, no arc, no touch, just a straight heave at the rim. He started running after each ricocheting ball, but soon gave that up and walked. Sometimes he took breaks to look at his phone, which he'd placed on a towel at the far end of the court.

None of it looked like much fun, and barely like physical activity, but it was more than I was doing. I spent the majority of my life sitting, and it was beginning to show. I was starting to sag into the shape of a man hunched over a wheel. I was too fucking young for that. After another twenty minutes of me telling myself I'd start doing something, running, swimming, yoga, anything to exercise, as soon as this was over, as soon as I stopped working at the energy-draining, soul-crushing warehouse and more time to get my shit together, after telling myself all that, he got in his car and drove. Around noon he parked at the assisted living complex and was there for about two hours, then home and around dinnertime he was back at the complex.

I let this play out another day. I sawed the broom handle into two pieces about a foot long each and attached about the same length of wire to connect the handles. That went back into the bag in the trunk.

I played it out in my mind at work, and tried not to think about it too much, just figure out the how and when, concentrate on the wire and how securely it was attached to the broom, think of the saw that cut them and the sawdust, think of the warehouse and the door somewhere in the distance that opened outside for the last time.

I worked quickly without rushing; I worked through lunch and hoped that there wouldn't be an accident or spill at the end of the day. I had to leave. I waited until the last minute and then drove straight to the assisted living parking lot. I wasn't sure if I was going to make it. I tried not to speed from the warehouse into town, but I had to step on it. I remembered Frank and Timothy McVeigh and his expired registration. Son of Sam and a parking ticket. You have to concentrate on the little things.

It was dark in the parking lot, with pools of electric light on dark pavement, trying to fill empty parking spaces, and a few cars, old Cadillacs and Continentals mostly, parked for good maybe. I pulled next to one near the end of the lot, close to the exit. I got the bag out of the trunk and got into the back seat. I changed my clothes and shoes and put on the coveralls. I put the wired broom handles in the front of the coveralls and walked to his car. He never locked it. I had checked it every time. He never locked it. I got into the back seat and waited. It wouldn't be long.

It was too long.

I could smell him in the car; I could smell his hair and sweat, his shaving cream and toothpaste; his deodorant and Tiger Balm he probably rubbed on his shoulder after all those shitty shots at the baskets. I thought about the kid in the house at the bottom of the stairs. He wasn't breathing. I thought about who might have come in after me and what the kid told them and why they would have killed him anyway. I thought about the kid and how he'd never get any older, not old enough to tell anybody anything ever again, not old enough to get mixed up in any of the awfulness that surrounded him and took him down. I thought about Frank walking from that same house, wondering if he knew what was going to happen to him when he turned the corner. I thought about him lying there in the basement of the hospital, lying on the street, waiting to be found. I thought about who he was and who he would never be again. I thought I might throw up. I thought I would have to get out. The car was so small and getting smaller. I thought I couldn't do it.

Then the door opened and closed and I didn't have to think at all. I only had to act.

IIIII

I went back to my car and took a large garbage bag out of the trunk. I took off my shoes and coveralls and gloves and put them in the bag and put the bag in the trunk. I would burn them later, along with the clothes I was wearing. I would cut the steel wire into tiny pieces and put it in with the clothes and the broom handles all of it in the fire.

I drove home and went directly to the shower. Afterward I flossed my teeth, staring intently at each tooth and the thread moving back and forth between them. I kept my mind focused on what I was doing. The gum started to bleed between the canine and an incisor, the blood washing over the teeth. I let the cold water run until it got as cold as it could get, then filled my mouth with cold water and let it stay there for a moment. I spat it into the sink and then brushed, carefully and deliberately. It was all the same. It was the same as the night before and the night to come. Tomorrow I would get up and go back to work and tomorrow night come home and stand in front of the same mirror in the same bathroom and go about the same business. That's all I had to think about.

I went to the couch and read a few pages in a book Casey had given me. It was about scientists studying fruit flies. They were creating mutant fruit flies and putting them in glass jars and watching them, hoping to find out about genetics and behavior. Other scientists were doing the same thing with fungus and bacteria. I read about how after millions of years of evolution, we still share the same genes as fruit flies and fungus and bacteria. It's all the same. I tried to only think about fruit flies and the fact that atoms are not alive and we're nothing but atoms and maybe none of us are alive, not really, more like puppets moved by these particles that control us, like flies and fungus and bacteria. I tried to think about that. But twisting through every sentence on every page was the thought of the empty bed in the other room, and the thought about Frank and what I had done and hadn't done and how nothing was the same.

28
THE CRASH

CASEY WANTED TO HELP, SO I LET HER.

"I want to find the driver, the guy who hit us," I told her. "Can you see if an ambulance went to the scene, maybe if someone went to the emergency room, anything like that?"

Casey said she could look into it.

She had access to the hospital records, I guess. It took a few days but she came back with a short list of names.

"I think it's this one," she said, pointing to the top name. "Young guy, was treated for a broken nose and a dislocated shoulder the night of the accident. He fits the bill, anyway."

"And the others?"

"Similar profile, same night, car accidents, but older. I figured I'd include everything, just in case the first one isn't a match."

|||||

After work, I went to the first address and waited. I was waiting for Daniel Dupont, a name that meant nothing to me, so I searched for anything about him. Twenty-something who didn't have a regular job, it seemed, who rented an apartment in the address I had. Casey was probably right about him. He fit the bill. I found some photos and social media posts, what he ate and where, where he had a drink or two, nothing interesting.

I ate the Chinese food I'd picked up after work, a carton of fried rice and chicken with snow peas. A couple of hours later the car still smelled like the food, maybe more so. I cracked a window and hoped for a breeze. There wasn't one. I grabbed the take-out bag from the backseat and fished for a fortune cookie. I couldn't read the small print in the dark of the car and didn't feel like turning a light on. I thought I could make out enough of the words. "The world is not meaningful, nor absurd. That's what's so remarkable about it." Something like that.

It was about ten o'clock when Dupont came out of the house and got in his car. I followed him as he drove through the back streets for a while. He drove like a guy who thinks he's being followed, or doesn't want to be followed. I wasn't sure if I cared that he knew I was behind him or not. I kept trailing him, staying about a half block behind until he parked. I was at an intersection and turned the corner, went around the block, and parked behind him, almost a full block behind him. He hadn't gotten out of the car. He never did. He sat in the car for hours.

I wondered if Dupont was working for Froehmer, watching a target the way I did. Maybe Mobley had taught him my tricks. Maybe Froehmer. I could see his silhouette in the driver's seat; it felt like I was watching the person I used to be. Then, every few minutes, a cloud of smoke would stream out of the driver's window. Dupont was smoking or vaping or whatever, but definitely calling attention to himself. He hadn't been taught much, it turned out, or not enough. Maybe he just didn't learn.

I hoped that someone would call the cops on him, had thought about calling them myself, but I sat there and watched Dupont sit there and watch until almost morning, then he drove off and I followed.

He pulled into a fast food place and parked and went inside. I waited until he got his food; I watched him through the window as he got his food and sat at a table. He had a large soda, a breakfast sandwich and a packet of hash browns. I went in and sat across from him.

When he saw me, he started to get up, but I grabbed him by the wrist and told him it was all right. "Go ahead and eat," I said and he sat back down.

"You know who I am?" I said.

"No."

"I'm Jerry Caldwell."

"No you're not."

"No, I'm not, but I work for him, the same as you."

"I don't think so."

"My partner and I were hired by a guy who uses the name Jerry Caldwell to go pick up something for him, then, when we have it, you crash into us, with a car rented by a guy who uses the name Jerry Caldwell. What do you suppose that's all about?"

"I never met the man," Dupont said.

"You just drove the car."

"That's right."

"You don't know this man?" I showed him a picture of Froehmer.

"Total stranger."

"You know what happened to my partner?"

He shook his head.

"He was murdered a few hours after you hit us. I'm just trying to figure out what happened to him."

"I was in the hospital," Dupont said.

"I know you were. I just want to know what you were doing and who for."

He took a long drink on his soda and leaned back in his chair. "I know this guy. And he asks me if I want to do an easy job, that all I have to do is find you and your partner on a certain day and take something from you. He said it wouldn't be a problem."

"So you ran into us."

"I've done it before."

"Where? *Grand Theft Auto*?"

"I've seen it done," Dupont said.

"Maybe in the movies," I said. "It had to work better there."

"I forgot the airbags," he said. As if that were the only thing that had gone wrong.

"But you don't know the guy in the picture?"

"Never saw him. I never saw anybody. The guy I know set it up for me. I talked to a guy on the phone. He told me there was a car under the Caldwell name and my guy set it up so I could go and pick it up. They tipped me off that you had the thing, and I tried to get it. Then I had to call my guy and tell him what had happened. He wasn't happy." He leaned forward and took another drink of his soda.

"And that's it? Do you think you were talking to Caldwell on the phone?"

"I don't know."

I ran through a bunch of other names Frank had created for Froehmer. I threw Froehmer's name at him, and Mobley's. He'd heard none of them. It didn't mean anything. "I don't remember the name," Dupont said. "But it wasn't any of those. I don't think it was your guy. I think it was someone else."

"Why's that?"

"My guy said that three or four people were after the same thing. That I wouldn't have much time to get it. That's why I did what I did. He said someone was going to wind up with it, and it better be me."

"You're working off a debt for that, I bet."

"I'm working it off. What happened to the thing?"

"Someone's got it," I said, "But it's not you, and it's not me."

I wasn't sure I'd gotten anywhere, just further around the circle I'd been going round in my head over and over. I wasn't sure if Dupont was telling me the whole truth, but he seemed harmless enough and I didn't have any more use for him. I was wrong on both counts.

29
THE MOVE

SOMEONE WAS FUCKING WITH ME.

I came home from work one night and there was a bowl and a spoon on the kitchen counter I know wasn't there when I left. They had been in the dish drainer. I know this.

The third time, there were drugs left on the counter. I didn't know if Mobley (or Froehmer or Dupont or whoever) wanted me to take the drugs, or if it was a warning that they could plant something on me, put the cops on me whenever they wanted. It was a test; it was a message; it was a small amount of meth. I would like to say that I got rid of it immediately. I did not. I hid it in the car. I kept saying it was a last resort. If I couldn't stay awake, if all else failed.

The fourth time there was a gun on the counter. My first thought was that it was the gun used to kill the kid and now the murder weapon was in my apartment. I had to get rid of it. But then, if it was the murder weapon, maybe I should hang on to it. I didn't know what to do. Or maybe it had nothing to do with the kid. Maybe I was going to need the gun, maybe that was the message. Mobley (or Froehmer or whoever) had put it there for me to use real soon. I got it out of the apartment, but I didn't get rid of it. I put it some place safe, but nowhere that could be tied to me.

The next day, the whole apartment was tossed, but not really. Every cabinet door and every dresser drawer, kitchen drawer, anything that could open, was open. Nothing appeared out of place, but they wanted me to know that they had looked, or could look. I knew what they were looking for. They could bring in a hundred guys and tear the place down to the studs; they could bring in a thousand bloodhounds and the best forensic teams and they'd never find a trace. What they were looking for had never been there. I'd locked the trophy in a safe I'd rented. There was so much distance between me and the thing that they'd never find it without my help. But I was tired of Froehmer or whoever it was he'd sent with their messages. I figured I'd send one of my own.

In the small hours of the morning, I got up from the couch and boxed up everything I wanted, my clothes and books, and Frank's clothes and books and I went out to the street just out of cautious paranoia and looked to see if anyone was watching me, the way I would. The street was empty. So I loaded up the car with boxes and drove away. Let them come and go as they pleased. They wouldn't find anything. Let them leave another message; there wouldn't be anyone to get it. If they wanted to find me, they knew where I was, but they weren't going to know where I lived. They could play their games with a ghost, but not with me.

I called Casey and told her that people had been harassing me. "Come stay with me," she said, without any hesitation.

"That's not what I was fishing for," I told her.

"Stay anyway," she said. "Stay for a night or for a week, a month, as long as you need."

IIIII

Casey had an extra bedroom, but I stayed on the couch. "I can't sleep in a bed," I told her. "Not yet, anyway." I gave Frank's things to Casey; she kept them in the boxes they came in, stacked in her bedroom. "You might still want them back," she said. I kept my boxes stacked between the end of the couch and the wall. "You can at least use the closet in the other room," Casey said. I didn't. I didn't know how long I would be there. I was more restless than I thought I would be, no matter how comfortable Casey tried to make things.

IIIII

After a week or so, we fell into a rhythm. I worked regular hours and came and went at predictable intervals. Casey's schedule was more erratic—she was gone for long stretches some days, then would come home and sleep for a few hours and then go back to the hospital—but she was around enough that we could have dinner together and then watch TV before the day ended. She never asked me questions. She never talked about Frank unless I talked about him first. She never talked about anything personal unless I initiated it. She talked about her work, or things in the news. "We didn't have to do surgery after all," she told me about a patient she'd been worried about. Or, "There used to be twelve different types of elephants, now there are only three. You know why a land animal can't get as big as a whale? Gravity." She knew what to say; she was distracting me. We were good distractions for each other. I slept better on Casey's couch (which was at least three inches too short for me to stretch out on) then I had in a long time. We had developed our own patterns and rhythms and part of that was going to meetings. I went to her meetings.

I never said much, but listened to the families of addicts talk about the trauma and impact on their lives. I could hear Casey talk with Frank's same words, with her similar face, and its easy pleasantness, but her words wouldn't reach people the way Frank could; she couldn't make them work the way Frank could. People heard Casey; they would nod their heads and agree, but they wouldn't listen, wouldn't let the words work on them and affect them the way they did when Frank said the same things. It was the same message, but the messenger made the difference. I didn't want it to be that way; I wanted Casey to connect; I wanted people to listen to her and absorb the good things she was saying, but it rarely happened. I never said anything to her.

"You should see me with kids," she might say after a meeting where we could see people drifting away as she spoke. "I'm good with kids."

"We should find a meeting with kids in recovery," I told her. "I'd go."

Casey was standing talking with a small group of people after a meeting when the leader of that night's meeting came up to me. I was exhausted, still working at the warehouse and just after I'd finished the job for Froehmer. I probably looked like shit, that's what set the guy off, I'm sure, but he caught me off guard.

"I hope you keep coming. But I don't know how much good we can do for you right now. We can't get you sober, but we can help you stay that way," he said. He was confused.

"You might have me mistaken for someone else," I said.

"I know who I'm looking at," he said. "I hope I see you again."

"You don't know who you're looking at," I said. "You don't know anything about me."

"I know you," the guy said. "That's all I'm saying. I hope we see you again."

I stopped going with Casey. I tried to avoid her on the nights she was going to go. She never said anything. She was good that way, and it made me feel worse.

"I have to find my own group," I finally told her. "I heard that from someone."

"Frank?"

"No, you," I told her.

30
THE SECOND

I WAS STILL WORKING AT THE WAREHOUSE, STILL DRIVING AROUND IN MY ORANGE VEST PICKING UP GARBAGE AND CLEANING UP MESSES. Froehmer would keep me there now, keep everything the same, even though I wanted to go back to what I'd been doing before. I began to wonder if I'd ever leave the warehouse. At least my paycheck meant something now. But not much. I could pay the bills and still scrape together a little something for child support, but that was about it. I didn't need much, but I needed more than this. My nose was above water, but not by much. I was working harder than ever, and making less. I could feel the vise of the working life, and I didn't like it. Then Froehmer called.

He wanted to meet at the diner. I got there a good half hour before we were supposed to meet and sat with my face toward the door, so I could see him come in. I didn't know what he wanted to talk about and sat wondering why he wanted a face-to-face. All my thoughts led to something not good. I shouldn't have thought about it.

Froehmer sat down across from me and nodded, pleased that I had been early. "How are you holding up?" he asked. "Good."

"Not your first choice of work, the warehouse, but you're doing all right?" It wasn't necessarily a question.

"I'm good," I said.

"We'll try to get you out of there when we can, on to something better," he said. "Unless you're happy where you are."

"I could use a change."

"Where are you living now?"

"I'm staying with a friend," I told him. "Something closer to work. Until I find a place of my own."

"Don't go looking out there yet," he said. "It might be temporary. I'm working on it." I nodded. "It's too bad you didn't keep your dad's place," Froehmer said.

"I couldn't afford it, not at the time. Not now, even."

"You take after your mother like that," he said. "She could spend a dime when your father brought home a nickel."

"I did all right once I got out of the hole," I said.

"You're out of another one," Froehmer said. "Your dad would be happy about that."

I wondered. I wondered if he would be happy.

"Anyway," Froehmer said, "I wanted you to know that I haven't forgotten about you. I'm working on improvements." He took a forkful of food from his plate. "You never can tell," he said.

"Never tell what?"

“The way they cook in this place.” Another forkful. “Hang in there, things will come around. You’re doing good. Good things will follow.”

“I’m hanging in there,” I said. Froehmer reached across the table between us and put his hand on my shoulder. “I see your dad in you, but I see you too,” he said. “Know that I’m thinking about you, that I see you, and where you could be.” I nodded and he got up and left me with the check.

When I got back to my car, Mobley was sitting in the passenger seat. “How’d that go?” he said.

“Good.”

“I’ve got a way for you to make some money,” he said. “Some real money.”

“How much?”

Mobley told me a number and I shook my head and told him a number. It was Mobley’s turn to shake his head.

“Putin gave a guy three thousand dollars,” he said.

“And a car, an expensive car. I don’t want the car; I want the cash. Or you can find the guy who’ll do it for the three.”

Mobley acted as if he was thinking about it, as if he had any part of the decision. I knew Froehmer had already given him a ceiling and I figured it was probably twice what Mobley had offered. I told him another number, a much larger number. “I can’t do that,” he said. “You know the Russian never got to drive the car. Or spend the money.”

I suppose it was a threat.

“We should talk to Froehmer,” I said.

“That’s not going to happen.”

“Then I’ll call him.”

Mobley took the phone out of my hand. “That’s not how it’s going to work. You know that.”

We sat in silence for a few moments while Mobley probably tried to figure out how he could still steal a few dollars from my end. Maybe he figured it out finally, or maybe he gave up trying. I didn't care. "I'll get your ask," he said. It was the only time I ever negotiated anything, and I'm sure I came up short. I got what I asked for. Or close enough to it, but I should have asked for more. It was my first negotiation, but I didn't think it would be my last.

Mobley handed back my phone and gave me a photo of the target and some information scribbled in pencil on the back. Mobley opened the door and got out. Just as he was closing the door I said, "That's the last time you sit in my car."

He grabbed the door and stopped it from closing.

I couldn't see Mobley but I could see the door hanging in the air, waiting for him to do something, waiting for him to say something. He slammed the door shut and started to walk away, but couldn't let it go. He opened the door but didn't lean down, his face was above the car somewhere in the dark, his mouth moving.

"The job comes first," he said, "but afterwards, we'll have business together."

Mobley closed the door and left. I didn't care what he said. He could threaten me all he wanted; he couldn't do anything. He couldn't do anything except what Froehmer told him, and Froehmer had me working. I was earning again and I felt good about myself. I hadn't felt like that in a while. It didn't last long. It never does, I guess. Not long enough, anyway. The future has nothing good.

I parked a block away from the house and waited for his car to pass me, then I got out and walked toward the house. He was still sitting in the car; I could see his dark silhouette in the driver's seat. I slowed my pace and waited for him to get out. He closed the car door and walked down the sidewalk, away from me and away from his house. Maybe he knew I was behind him, there in the dark, waiting for him.

I stopped and thought about going home, calling it off for the night. He continued on down the sidewalk, which dipped down a slope, and if I was going to keep going, I had to keep him in sight, not let him get on the other side of the slope. So I started walking again, almost against my better judgment, almost against my own will.

There were lights on in his house, but the curtains were drawn. It was that way all up and down the block. Maybe there was someone home waiting for him, maybe a whole family. I didn't know; I didn't want to know. I tried not to think about it. I tried to concentrate on the small shadow in front of me.

I quickened my pace. I didn't walk hard and I didn't walk fast, but he could hear me behind him. I could hear his shoes stutter step on the concrete and I knew he could hear me. I didn't walk faster, but kept pace with him, his silhouette the same distance ahead of me, moving down the slight hill. I could have caught up with him, but I thought I'd wait until he went up the other hill. Or if he turned back, he'd have to come up the hill toward me. I thought I knew what I was doing. I thought I had it figured out.

He was at the bottom of the hill and I quickened my pace. He kept walking, not changing his speed. It would be better like this, better for Froehmer. He wanted a message and he'd get one, left there on the sidewalk for everyone to see. I had shortened the distance between us to maybe twenty feet when a car came down the street behind me. I moved off the sidewalk and tried to stay in the dark. But he was lit up for longer than I would have liked. I didn't want to see him. I didn't want to see his worried face as he looked back toward the car. He was almost asking for help, but the car kept on going, returning us both to the dark, with only the dim lights from the houses, pulled tight behind their curtains.

He stopped at the corner and stood under a streetlight and waited. I thought he was daring me to do it right there, but I stayed in the shadows. He looked at his watch and I didn't move. After a few minutes a car came and my target got in and the car drove off. It was all unusual.

I ran up the hill thinking I could beat the car back to his house, but I had no idea where they were going.

No one had beaten me. No one had come, no one was coming.

I hid in a clump of dark bushes, hemlock or yew or some shit like that, some clump in the neighbor's yard where I could stand and watch for him. The lights went out in the windows and I still waited. I stood there for almost two hours and the more I stood there the more I thought I was an idiot, the more I knew I was one. Maybe it would be better to break into his house and wait, I thought, where no one could see me standing there in the bushes. I could wait for him in his own house. Maybe I'd be waiting there for days. Maybe I'd fall asleep and the wife or kids or whoever else was in the house would find me and call the cops. It was better to be in the bushes, but how long could I stand there? I'd missed my chance and he'd gone off somewhere safe. I would have some explaining to do. Maybe he would never come back.

I wasn't cut out for this type of work. The doubts and the second-guessing began to pile up and I thought I should go home and regroup when a car pulled in front of his house and the target got out. The car drove off without waiting for him to get inside the house. They never knew I was there. He never knew I was following him. I'd been wrong about it all from the start. But that was okay. I made my way across the black lawn, with my knife out and ready. I had him just before he got to the front door and did the work Froehmer wanted. He let out a gasp when I got next to him, but he wasn't afraid. Not for long anyway. I killed him with one blow, like a sheep.

I hurried through the yards and made a roundabout way back to my car, spending as little time on the street as possible. No one saw me. I knew that much. It was done, and the doing of it wasn't the trouble. I never imagined myself in this position; I never imagined that I'd ever have to kill someone in my entire life. But then soldiers probably think the same thing. Maybe cops too. Or maybe that's all they think about. I never had. I had justified what I'd done before, stealing. No one ever got hurt, not really. Now I had killed two people in less than three months, and had a third hanging over me. It wasn't the killing that bothered me. It was the time before and the time after, the time when I had to think about it, think about who I had become and how I got here. I thought about the guy dead on the sidewalk and if it was the message Froehmer wanted. I'd have to avoid the news for the next few days.

I liked the jobs where there weren't any people around to screw up everything. But those days were gone. Froehmer had different ideas now. All I could hope was that he would make it worth my while. And he did. Mobley handed me an envelope. It was more money than I'd ever seen at once. I think even my father would have been impressed.

31
THE MOTHER

SHE WAS ON THE PORCH BEFORE I COULD GET OUT OF THE CAR. So I sat and waited as she walked the short walkway from the house to the curb. She didn't want me inside. It was her mother's house. So I stayed put.

I had texted her to see if I could come over. I don't know the last time we'd had a conversation. She'd left me a few messages about child support, but I'd ignored them. I didn't have any money. Now I did. Now I could do something for the kid. That's why I'd wanted to come over, but I wasn't sure what to say. She sat in the passenger seat and let me try to figure it out.

"How's Eva?" I said.

"Real good."

"Sixth grade?"

"Too smart for the sixth grade," she said.

"She inside?"

"She has science club after school."

I had told her I wanted to see Eva. That's why I'd come after school. I tried to let it go. "What happens in science club?"

She shrugged. "I don't know. I think they're building a weather balloon or something this project. It's over my head, I know that."

"Mine too, I'm sure," I said. "How's your mother?"

"She's good. Helping out a lot, where she can. She's inside. You want to go see her?"

I knew she wasn't serious.

"She still mad at me?"

"She'll always be mad at you."

"She has her reasons."

"We all have our reasons," she said.

I handed her an envelope and she took it and looked inside. "For Eva," I said.

She kept looking inside the envelope. "How much is in here?"

"About thirty-five." It was almost the entire payout from Froehmer. "Put it in the college fund, or the science club, whatever. But for Eva, you know."

"You need to get away from Froehmer," she said.

"It's all right," I said. "I'm doing all right."

"You need to get away from him."

"And do what?"

"If I were your age I think I'd bust my ass to get into a more dignified form of endeavor," she said in a voice I recognized.

"That's your mother talking."

"Not just to me, you know. You could do anything you want. You always could."

"It doesn't work like that. You know that. I'm ahead for the first time in a long time, and I'm going to stay ahead for a while."

"I hope so," she said. "But be careful. And look out, you know. I mean it."

"Froehmer looks out for me. He always has."

"He looks out for himself, and that's it. You need to do the same."

"I'm trying," I said. "How about you?"

"I'm looking out for Eva. That keeps me in line. I might even go back to school. I don't know. We could take classes like we used to."

IIIII

"When's science club over with?"

"Not for a while," she said. "I should get back inside before my mother thinks you've kidnapped me."

"I'm not going to see Eva?"

"Next time," she said. "I'll have to figure it out."

"What's to figure out?"

She folded the envelope and pushed it down into her pocket. She turned and looked at me and said, "I'm going to say goodbye before this turns into a fight. Thanks for the help. We'll see about next time."

She closed the door on me and I walked back to my car. I was standing in the street, fishing for my keys, when I saw a car coming up the street towards me. It put on the brakes hard and stayed in the street for a moment. I couldn't see who was driving, but there was somebody in the passenger's seat I thought I recognized. It was Eva.

She got out of the car and made her way to the sidewalk and walked toward me. The car did a U-turn and drove off.

"Who was that?" I said.

"Mom's boyfriend," Eva said.

"Why'd he leave you in the street?"

Eva shrugged. "He had to go, I guess."

"You want to go get an ice cream?"

Eva got in the car and we drove off. I didn't tell her mother.

"How long has your mom had a boyfriend?"

"A long time," Eva said. "I mean he's back now, I guess. He was away for a while."

"Out of town?"

"I don't know," she said. "He said he's known me my whole life. But I don't remember him. I only remember him from the past few weeks or so."

"And you like him?"

"He's all right. He says he knows you. I miss Frank," she said.

"I miss Frank too. Wait. He knows me? What's his name?"

"Moe," Eva said.

"Moe Szyslak?"

Denise texted me. "WTF," she wrote. "Bring her home. NOW."

I texted back, "On our way."

"Not that Moe."

Denise texted back, "NOW."

"Does he have a bar?"

"It's not that Moe," Eva said.

"I don't know any other Moe," I said.

"Maybe you don't know him," Eva said. "But maybe you will. You should meet him."

"I could have," I said. "But he drove off. Had to get to his bar, I guess."

"That's not him."

"Sure sounds like him," I said.

I pulled up in front of Eva's house. Denise was on the porch, waiting to explode on me. I didn't get out of the car. She gave me a nice finger and I waved back before I drove off.

32
THE MEETING

I WENT TO A MEETING. Talking to Denise had made me want to take something, anything, just a little whatever to knock everything down a notch or two, erase it for a while. I hadn't felt like that in a long time. Not the momentum that goes from an urge to an action, an action you tell yourself that you can manage, just once, or just once in a while, but ends up managing you. I never felt like that. Which is why I went to a meeting. It didn't make me feel better, but it kept me from regretting at least one decision.

It was a large group, and I sat near the front and listened to everyone as they told their stories. They're all the same, for the most part. I try to be sympathetic – I am sympathetic – but they're all clichés, really.

I'm a cliché, I suppose. But at least I kept my mouth shut. I sat and listened and nodded my head, and applauded whenever everybody else did, but the time in the room was for me, and it gave me what I wanted without having to stand up and say anything.

As I was leaving, somebody came up next to me and said, "Can we talk." It was the neighbor I'd talked to when I was asking about Frank. The one who was using when I talked to him; the one I said a bunch of stuff to I shouldn't have. The one the cops asked me about. The guy I told them I didn't know, because I didn't know his name. Robert Bowie. I hardly recognized him.

"Sure," I said, "for a minute."

"We should go someplace," he said. "You're in trouble. I want to help."

We walked to a park a few blocks away and stood on a corner. I could see down the block and through the park, and tried to look around as often as possible to look up and down in all directions. "Let's go in there," he said and motioned toward the park. I didn't move.

"You nervous?" he said.

"Shouldn't I be?"

"Yes," he said. "But not about me. I'm here to help. No one knows I'm here."

I followed him into the park and we moved off the path and sat on a bench. He sat; I stood and tried not to pace.

"They're coming for you," he said.

"Who?"

"I don't know exactly. I'm not supposed to know, I guess. And neither are you. But they know you have it, and they want it now."

"I don't have it."

"We both know that's a lie. Everybody knows."

"Because the kid told you and you told everybody."

"It wasn't supposed to happen that way."

"And how was it supposed to happen?"

"They told me that a guy was running stuff out of that house and that if I took it from him, it would be worth my while. That's what I was told. So I waited and watched the house, and when I saw it was you going in, I didn't know what to do. I froze. Then the kid went in, and I really didn't know what to do. So I did nothing."

"That's not true. You shot him. You roughed him up first. You didn't have to do that."

"I didn't do that. I went in and he was sitting on the stairs. He looked in bad shape. I wanted to know what had happened, that's all. Maybe you hadn't taken the stuff. I didn't know. So he was on the stairs, trying to get himself together it looked like. I figured you'd beaten him and took off, but before I could ask him anything, he came at me, charged at me. He would have killed me, that's how he looked. So I shot him. I was never supposed to use the gun. They told me that all I had to do was put it in your face and you'd hand over the bag. I screwed up, but they said they could make it work. That's what happened."

"Who do you work for?"

He shrugged.

"What happened to the gun?"

"It wasn't mine. I gave it back to the guy who gave it to me."

I described Froehmer to him. It wasn't Froehmer. I described Mobley to him. It wasn't Mobley. Or at least that's what he had me believe. I didn't know how much to believe of anything.

"You don't know who you work for any more than I do, not really," he said. "I was brought into this because of you, and that's why I'm bringing this to you. You be careful. I don't want you to wind up like your friend."

"Do you know who killed my friend?"

He shook his head. "I don't know anything, but I know this is bigger than we know. There are at least three people after that trophy," he said. "It could be any of them."

"I need to know."

"I can't help you with that. I just did a job. I didn't know it was you. I got caught up in something that was supposed to be easy, and I screwed it all up. That's why I'm here. They've got me in a box. You know that now. You know what it's like. You know how that works. I'm telling you something to help. You need to hand it over. You don't know how bad things can get."

"I've got an idea of it," I said. "Maybe I'll just get rid of it, for once and for all. Then nobody will have it. There will be nothing to come for."

"You know it won't work like that. Give it to whoever hired you, if he can protect you. Otherwise they're coming."

"They'll come either way, I suppose."

"I suppose."

"How'd you find me?"

"It wasn't so hard," he said.

"Then what took you so long?" I was joking, but he answered anyway.

"I was away for a while. And it took me some time to sort things out. I couldn't pin the kid on you. I couldn't do that."

"It could come back on you."

"It could. I'm guilty of it. I'm guilty."

"We're all guilty," I said. "My friend Frank used to say that all you could do was just to live and be guilty."

"I guess that's true."

"You know I wasn't running stuff, right?"

"I know that. Now."

"You know what I got out of it?"

He shook his head.

"The same as you. Nothing. So far. But I'll get something for myself out of it, maybe something for the both of us."

It didn't matter. I didn't have time to get anything done. It was done to me first.

33
EVA

I TRIED TO DO SOMETHING RIGHT AND ALL IT DID WAS CAUSE MORE WRONG. Two days after I gave Denise the money, I got an anonymous text. "How's Eva?" I didn't respond, but called Denise right away. She was worried. Eva hadn't come home from school. No one knew where she was.

"Someone's got her," I said and told her about the text. She wanted to call the police. It took a lot of convincing to stop her and I wasn't sure she wouldn't still call later. "I'll get her back," I told her. "They won't do anything to her. They just want something from me. I'll take care of it."

"Who's they?" she said, but she didn't really want to know. "It's Froehmer, isn't it?"

"It's not Froehmer." And that conversation went on longer than it should have.

"I should call the police," she said near the end.

"Give me some time before that," I told her again. "I'll get her back soon. I promise. Just give me a little time."

I texted back. "What do you want?"

"You have something."

"What?"

"Goat."

"I don't have it. I swear."

"Then get it. For Eva."

And that was it. They didn't respond to more texts from me. I sat around and thought about what to do. I didn't think about it long enough. I called Froehmer and told him that I had to see him, that it was urgent.

We met a couple of blocks from the diner. I got into the backseat of Froehmer's car. Froehmer was in the passenger seat, and Mobley was driving. "Somebody's got Eva," I told him "And I need to find out who it is."

"What do they want?"

"Something I don't have. That trophy from a while back. You think it's the people who hired you? You think you could talk to them?"

"It doesn't work like that," Froehmer said. "They wouldn't do that."

"Then who?"

"Give me some time," Froehmer said.

"I don't have time," I told him.

"What do you want me to do, then?"

"Tell them I don't have the thing."

"I don't know who they are," Froehmer said.

"Just tell them."

"Maybe you should give them what they want," Mobley said.

"And maybe you're not as smart as you think," I said.

"Don't judge his brains by yours," Froehmer said. He was talking to Mobley, but Mobley was dumb enough to think Froehmer was talking to me.

"I don't have it," I told them both. "He's always on me about this," I told Froehmer, "and he doesn't know what he's talking about."

"And now someone else thinks you have it," Froehmer said.

"Maybe Mobley knows who it is," I said. He turned back and for a moment I thought he was going to come over the seat after me. I wish he would have.

"I didn't even know you had a kid," Mobley said. "All I know is you never finished that job. It all went south because of you and your partner."

"If I had it, I'd have given it to you," I said. "I'd have given it to you a long time ago. And you know I don't have it; you've been through all my stuff."

Mobley was going to say something but Froehmer cut him off. "This is about the girl," he said. "This is about getting her back. Give me a couple of hours. Let me see what I can find out. That's all I can do for now."

I drove back to Casey's and was happy that she wasn't home. I tried to wait for Froehmer to call, but couldn't just sit around. I got back in the car and drove around. Finally, Froehmer called. He didn't have anything. "It has to be someone you know," I told him. "How many people could connect me to that job?"

"Maybe it comes back to Frank," he said. "Maybe he talked about it. You should work that end." Froehmer was done working on it. I should never have called him. I only wanted to know who it was before I did what I should have done from the start.

"I have it," I texted and attached a generic image of a trophy. All they had to do was open the image and a small piece of code would be on the phone and I could find whoever it was. There were easier ways to go about it, I know, but that's the way Frank had taught me.

"Let's get together," they texted back. "Will arrange soon."

I asked them to send me a picture of Eva, but they ignored me. It didn't matter. They'd opened the image. It was fucking Mobley. He sat there and lied to me. "I didn't even know you had a kid," he'd said. Fucking Mobley. He was freelancing and now I had to do something about it.

I thought about going right back to Froehmer, but maybe he was behind it. Maybe Denise was right about him. "I didn't even know you had a kid," Mobley said. Was that true? Froehmer knew; he'd known for years. But maybe Mobley didn't know. Maybe he didn't know it until I led him right to her. Somebody had followed me. I hadn't been careful enough and now they had Eva. I figured it had to be more than just Mobley. He couldn't pull it off on his own. I tried to think who else it could be. It didn't matter for the moment; I had him. All I had to do was keep tabs on him. Mobley wouldn't have Eva but he'd know where she was, and he'd check in on things now and then. I knew how it was going to work, or how they thought it would.

"I know who it is," I told Denise. "And I know what they want. All I have to do is give it to them and we'll get Eva back. I'll have her back soon, I promise. I'm just waiting to get instructions."

She wasn't relieved. But neither was I. There was still a lot that could go wrong.

"I'm not going to fuck this up," I told her.

It wasn't convincing, not even to me.

IIIII

I went and got a gun. Not the one that had been left for me. I needed something clean, so I went and bought one from someone who didn't know who I was, didn't care, and wouldn't care what I did with it. I got a pistol small enough to fit into my coat pocket. It held a magazine of eight and one in the chamber. I didn't know if I'd need more than that – I didn't know if I'd need it at all – but I bought a couple more magazines anyway. I hadn't fired a gun in years, not since I was in high school taking potshots at anything that moved out in the woods when we should have been doing something better. I didn't like the idea of even holding the thing, but I didn't know who I was going to find or what they were going to do when it came down to it. I didn't know what I was going to do. So like every other idiot, I bought a gun. It weighed less than two pounds in my pocket, fully loaded. It felt like a ton. I almost bought another one. I would have carried cannons if I thought that's what it would take.

|||||

I used to be afraid of Mobley, that stick of dynamite you knew could explode. But not anymore. I had the difference now. I knew where he was and how to find him and the kid. He wasn't going to stop me; he wasn't even going to get in the way. I had the difference.

|||||

I tried not to look at my phone every few seconds, but Mobley was on the move. He always was. That was his day, running around for Froehmer, or with him, always because of him, always at the end of his string. But not now. He would be on his own, sooner or later. I wanted to follow him, really follow him, get in the car and watch with my own eyes, but this way was better. I could look at the map and see where he was. Most of it was the usual spots, but he'd get to Eva eventually. I just hoped he'd get there before we'd made the final arrangements.

|||||

As soon as Casey saw me she knew I was in trouble.

"What's wrong?" she said.

I told her the whole thing, or most of it.

"You have to call the police," she said.

"They'll screw everything up," I told her. "It's easier this way. I give them what they want and get Eva back."

"What do they want?"

I told her.

"Why do you still have that?"

"I don't know," I said. "A lot of reasons, none of them any good."

"Like what?"

"Like I thought I might need it, that I could use it for something. Not like this, but for something else. Or the fact that it was the last thing Frank had, that we had together. I don't know. It all sounds stupid when I say it."

Casey didn't say anything. We sat at the table in her apartment and didn't say anything. Then she got up and went into her room. I thought she was done with me. I really did. Then she came back and sat at the table again.

"Have I told you the story about Frank and the watch?" she said.

I couldn't remember.

"Tell me," I said.

"Frank was at some party, a New Year's Eve party, I think. And there was some girl there flashing around an expensive watch she'd gotten for Christmas. At some point in the night, she dropped it, or it slipped off, or whatever, and was lying there on the couch. Frank went over and took it. The girl saw him do it, or thought she saw him, and told her boyfriend. When Frank was leaving, the boyfriend confronted him. 'I don't understand,' Frank said. You know him; he just stood there with that calm look on his face and denied it. 'You think I took it,' he said. There was a crowd around them and Frank was calm and the boyfriend was getting agitated. 'Just say you took it as a joke and we'll leave it at that,' the boyfriend said. 'But I didn't take it,' Frank said. 'And I can prove it.' He took off his coat and handed it the girl to inspect. He pulled everything out of his pockets and pulled out his pockets. There was no watch. 'I saw him take it,' the girl said. 'He doesn't have it,' somebody said, and the crowd turned against the girl. 'You want me to strip,' Frank said and started to unbutton his shirt. 'He doesn't have it,' somebody else said. Frank put on his coat and apologized to the girl. 'I'm sorry about your watch, but I had nothing to do with it. Maybe it was someone else. Maybe you lost it. I don't know. But I hope you find it. Happy New Year.' And he left."

"With the watch."

"The boyfriend and two other guys followed Frank and confronted him on the street. They demanded the watch and Frank still denied that he had it. They beat him up, beat him bad, and then went through his clothes. There was no watch.

"Frank came home all bloodied and I remember how unsympathetic my father was when Frank told him that three guys jumped him on the street. 'They didn't jump you for no reason,' he said. 'What did you do?' 'I didn't do anything,' Frank said. 'Then call the cops,' my father told him. He knew he wouldn't. My father thought Frank got what he deserved and that was that."

We sat in silence for a moment and then Casey said, "You're supposed to ask me about the watch."

"I know about the watch," I said. "Frank had it."

"You know the story."

"I know Frank."

Casey got up from the table again and went back to her room. When she came back she put an expensive watch on the table in front of me. "He gave it to me. He had it hidden in his underwear. He said he would have given it back if there hadn't been a crowd around him. He said he'd only taken it to trade for drugs, so he gave it to me. I wasn't even in high school then. I don't think he had ever given me anything. And here it was something that he'd stolen, that I knew he'd stolen and gotten beaten up for. And I took it and kept it all this time. I shouldn't have taken it, but I did. He gave it to me so I kept it. It was just between the two of us, you know; we were the only people in the world who knew about it. I hid it from my parents; I hid it from everyone. You're the only person I've ever shown it to, after all this time."

34
THE TROPHY

I HAD TO FIGURE OUT HOW TO GET IT BACK. I thought that every car that was behind me was following me. They had followed me to Eva's and now they were hoping I would take them to the thing they really wanted. I could keep an eye on Mobley, but he wasn't the one who would tail me. Mobley was at home; I spent the night looking at the stationary dot on the map on my phone, but I couldn't get the trophy from the safe until the morning. I spent the night looking at the dot and trying to think about how to get to the safe unnoticed. I had to go to work in the morning. I couldn't change my routine. I didn't know what to do.

The sun was almost up when Casey came out and saw me on the couch, staring at the phone. "You didn't sleep," she said.

"A little."

"I saw that blue light all night," she said. "When are you going to get her?"

"They haven't said yet. They're probably moving her first."

"Are you ready?"

"I have to get what they want, then I'll be ready."

"Where is it?"

"In a safe. I'm not sure how to get at it without them knowing."

"I'll get it," Casey said, without any hesitation. It was a solution, but not one that I wanted. I tried to talk her out of it; I tried to talk myself out of it, but I couldn't think of a better way for it to work.

"I can go this morning," she said.

I gave her the address and the combination for the safe. "It should be the only thing in the safe, but if it's not, it's a cardboard box, wrapped in red and blue duct tape. It's about this big," I said and held my hands up to show her the size.

"I'll get it and bring it back here."

I went outside and looked up and down the street. There were no cars waiting for me, no one camped out. I went out again in a couple of hours, right before I had to leave for work. No one. No one was going to follow me. No one was going to follow Casey. I was sure of it, as sure as I could be after having made a mistake, a big one. It would be over soon. One way or the other. And I was ready.

I went to work and tried to do my job, but hardly did much of anything except look at my phone. Mobley's dot was moving around in the familiar ways, controlled by Froehmer. It almost made me think he had nothing to do with any of it. But I knew that was wrong. And then he texted me, still anonymous. "Tomorrow. 5 am. Ready?"

"I'm ready."

"Instructions to come."

I called Denise. "I'll have her tomorrow morning."

"I still think we should call the cops."

"Tomorrow," I said. "If I don't have her tomorrow morning, call them. Can you wait that long?"

"No," she said, "but I will."

IIIII

When I got home from the warehouse, Casey was gone, but the cardboard box was on the table. I unwrapped it and looked at the trophy. "What people won't do for the dumbest things," Frank's voice said in my head.

I put the trophy in a bag and went to put the pistol (the one they'd left for me in my apartment) in next to it. I took the one I'd bought and practiced loading and unloading the clips. I did it with the three clips on the table, with the clips in my pockets, I even dropped them on the floor and tried to do it without looking. I tried not to think when I would have to do any of it; I just did it and then did it again and again. "Discipline is how you survive," someone had said in a meeting. I suppose it's true, but not necessarily. Some people survive on dumb luck, and some people with discipline can't make it very far. Discipline can only take you so far, no matter what. I put the gun in the pocket of my jacket and tried to stop thinking about it. I was eating something when Casey came home. She saw the bag and said, "Is it time?"

"I'm not sure yet," I said, "but I'll know soon."

"You'll give them what they want, right?"

I nodded and looked at the bag.

"Don't take chances on this. Okay?"

"I know," I said. "I'm thinking the way Frank would. No chances."

Casey looked at the bag. "Can I see what the fuss is all about?" I handed her the bag and watched her open it. There was a look of recognition on her face.

"Shit," she said.

"You know what that is?"

She nodded.

"Well? What is it?"

"The stuff that assholes are made of," she said.

"Don't be clever," I said. "Just tell me."

"It's a college sports thing," Casey said. "Lacrosse. It's a trophy a bunch of lacrosse assholes have been fighting over for about twenty years. You want to hear the whole story?"

"Not really. How do you know about it?"

"Frank. He was into lacrosse in high school for a while, really into it. Had pictures on the wall of some of these guys. He could have been a great player, but, well, you know the rest."

"But not all of it," I said. "He never told me any of this. None of it."

"Maybe he was trying to protect you," Casey said. "It had to be one of these guys who hired you, maybe that had something to do with it." She went on talking some more, but I wasn't listening. My phone lit up and when I looked I saw Eva's picture. Mobley had been dumb enough to send a picture. I looked at the map and saw he was outside of town a ways. He'd been there twice today. "I've got to go," I told Casey and grabbed the bag.

"I'm coming with you," she said.

"No," I said, "and I don't have time to talk about it."

"Don't talk then," she said and followed me to the car.

I let her get in and thought about it as we drove out. "You can't go with me," I said.

"I know," Casey said. "But I can be there when you get her. I'm good with kids, you know." I knew she was smiling. I didn't want to see it, not now. I looked over at her and tried not to think of what was about to happen.

I didn't know anyway, not yet.

|||||

We drove out to a small subdivision on a cul-de-sac, five houses that were all being built at the same time, none of them finished. They had the walls up and the roofs on, and most of the windows, ready for the wind and rain, and working inside when the winter came, if it ever did. There was a time when I would have been happy enough to go through those houses, pulling out anything I could, tools, copper, even leftover bricks and wood. I wasn't going back there, not now. We didn't go down the cul-de-sac, but drove past and found a utility road about half a mile away where you could see the backs of the houses, three of them anyway. We parked and Casey looked at the map. "Is he still there?" I asked her. "He's gone," she said. We couldn't be sure which house he'd been in, but it was good to have Mobley out of the way. Maybe he was gone for the night, not expecting me until the morning. I could only hope that no one was expecting me.

"Stay here and keep watching," I told her. "If you see Eva come out by herself, get her and take her with you. Don't wait for me."

"Does anyone ever listen to that?"

"Don't be like anyone else," I said. It was going to be dark soon and my better judgment told me to wait and approach the house in the dark. I didn't wait. I wanted to get Eva.

I grabbed the small black bag and opened it and handed the gun to Casey. I didn't know what to do with it, and she saw me hesitate. "I know my way around a gun," she said, "and I don't have any problem using it on anyone who would kidnap a kid." I looked at her; she was calm and her eyes were hard and strong and steady. "I mean it," she said.

"Maybe you should go and I'll stay here." It wasn't time for a joke.

"You know what you're doing," Casey said. "You've thought it through. You're going to go get your daughter."

"I'll get her."

I walked indirectly toward the houses, through a thin strand of trees that too quickly gave way to an unmowed meadow. I crouched down in the grass and kept an eye on the windows. I didn't see anyone in any of the houses, but that didn't mean anything. I was sure they could see me if they were watching, especially from a second floor in almost any of the houses. I knelt in the grass and scanned the five houses. I thought I saw a light come on in one of them, down low at the base of the house. It was hard to tell with the low light of the sun reflecting off some of the windows. I got up and ran toward the window where I thought there was a light.

I ran about a football field's worth of ground, maybe twenty seconds of running, the grass slowing me down, and the extra couple of pounds in the pocket of my jacket and the bag. I got close enough to see the light through the window, a bare bulb at the end of an extension cord hanging from the ceiling. I took the gun out of my pocket and waited for my breath to calm down. I didn't want to wait at all.

The room was empty, except for a plastic folding table and a couple of chairs. There were a couple of sodas on the table, and an open bag of potato chips. There was no Eva. I crouched and waited, hoping to see somebody, when suddenly somebody appeared in the room. They startled me and I didn't recognize them at first. I suddenly realized that I had no idea what to do. All the planning I had done in my head disappeared and I stood there in the dusk knowing I had no business trying to rescue Eva like this. It was as clear as the squares on the checkerboard, the way you know everything, the way you figure it all out in a snap second. I should play it the way they said. Give them what they want and hope they hand Eva over to me. I gripped the gun and tried to think it through, but before I could figure it out, the guy in the room turned and saw me and went to reach for something, I thought. I shot him as soon as he started. I think I hit him in the hip. I kicked out the screen and jumped down into the room.

The man was on the floor, clutching at his thigh, blood pooling underneath him. I checked to see if he had a gun, and when I leaned over him, he tried to get up and I shot him in his other leg. He went back to the concrete floor and turned and looked at me. I knew who he was. It was Daniel Dupont.

"Where's the girl?"

"There's no girl," he said. "You weren't supposed to be here. Not until tomorrow."

"Where's the girl?"

"There's no girl, dipshit. You were set up. Mobley and Denise, they set this up."

"What's she got to do with this?"

"Jesus. What you don't know. They're together, the two of them."

"And you."

"I'm not part of it," he said. "I was just helping out Mo."

It had been there right in front of me all this time. You look, but you don't see.

"And Froehmer?"

He shook his head. "Mobley." He tried to sit up but thought better of it. He put his head on the floor and still looked at me. I think I was still pointing the gun at him. "It's been going on a long time."

"Too long," I said. "He killed my partner over it."

"Froehmer did that," he said.

"No he didn't."

"Well, you know. Froehmer didn't put the needle in, but he got what he wanted. The way he always does. You know that much, right?"

Frank did right by him.

"Frank didn't listen. And you listened to Frank. And neither of you knew the way it worked." I showed him something in my face I didn't want him to see. "You don't have a clue."

"You can't figure them all," I said. "All I know is that I have something everyone else wants."

"And look where it's got you," he said.

"I don't want it," I said. "I never wanted it."

"But you still have it."

"It's right outside," I said. "Should I give it to you?"

"It doesn't matter," he said. "You know it doesn't. You can kill me right here, but that won't end it. You'll have to answer for it. You'll have to deal with Froehmer."

He was done talking. He closed his eyes and I shot him again. Then the floor hit me in the face.

IIIII

I saw the shadow charging at me just as I pulled the trigger, then Mobley crashed into me, tackling me to the floor. I dropped the gun somewhere and Mobley was on top of me, his weight pinning me deep into the concrete floor. He pressed his forearm into my windpipe and I tried to kick him off me. It was like trying to kick a pile of bricks. He had his weight on his left forearm, pushing it deep under my chin, while his right fist banged against my left ear. I tried to twist and kick and desperately tried to get an arm free, but he had me. I was still fighting, but it was getting hard to breathe, impossible to do anything. Mobley had me. My lungs were emptying out, my strength was leaving me. There was a dark pool floating just behind my eyes and I knew I was going to dive into it.

But I didn't. Two gunshots filled the room and Mobley stopped banging on my ear, stopped crushing my windpipe. His full weight slumped on top of me and I thought about going slack too, thinking that maybe a shot had been meant for me, but then I heard Casey. "Holy shit," she said.

I crawled out from under Mobley and had to stop and catch my breath. I was hunched over, not sure if I could stand up straight. Casey was shaking and crying and feeling the way someone should in that situation. I made my way to her and took the gun out of her hand. "I saw the car drive up," she said. "I didn't know what else to do. It was either him or you," she said, not looking at me. My throat hurt so bad I wasn't sure I could talk. "That's the only way to think about it," I said.

"Where's Eva?"

I shook my head. I couldn't do much more than that. She looked at me and saw all the blood on the front of my jacket. "Holy shit," Casey said.

I shook my head and tried to catch my breath again. "It's his." I took the gun from Casey and wiped it and put it near the dead guy, Dupont. My head hurt. My throat hurt. My shoulder hurt. I think everything hurt. Mobley had tagged me good. I took the other gun and wiped it clean and put it on the floor. I wasn't exactly sure which gun was supposed to go where. I wasn't exactly sure of anything except the pain in my shoulder and Casey standing there next to me. I looked at the room. Let the cops figure it out. They would have the murder weapon for the kid. Maybe they could put it together as far as that and leave the rest alone. It might keep us out of it. Or at least keep Casey out of it. That's all I needed. I could deal with the rest.

IIIII

We turned off the light in the room and made our way in the dark to the bag I'd left by the window, then went back to the car. I explained as much of it to Casey as I could. "Let's go home," she said. "We can sort it out later." I told her I wanted to see Denise. "And where would that lead?" Casey said. "Don't. Think about it first. Think about Eva." That's all it took.

Everything hurt worse than before. I could hardly lift my arm; my shoulder shot a deep depth-charge ache as I put my hand on the wheel. I wasn't sure I could drive. I wasn't sure I could go anywhere. But I did. I bit the inside of my cheek and kept my eyes on the road and tried not to think about the pain. I just needed to get into a bed somewhere and get Mobley to stop putting his fist into the side of my head and a hot iron into my shoulder. Another second or two and I would have been done, I thought. At least unconscious, concussed, and then he could have taken his time. I lowered the window and let the cool air find me.

"You want me to drive?" Casey said.

"Thank you. I'll be all right," I said. "I meant thank you for everything. Thanks for not listening, you know."

"I know."

She knew I wasn't going home, not yet. She grabbed the bag from the back seat and put it in her lap. "Can I look at it?" I nodded and she opened the bag and looked in, maybe just to convince herself what everything had been about. "Fuck them," she said.

"People who have everything fighting over nothing," I said.

I drove past Froehmer's house and saw his car in the drive. I parked a few blocks away and told Casey to stay put. "I mean it this time. I will be right back."

I was still sore but my head was clearing at least. I carried the black bag in my left hand and put my right hand in my coat pocket. It was empty except for two unused magazines. I thought about putting them in the bag, but didn't.

Every light was on in Froehmer's house. I'd been by his house a hundred times when I was a kid. We'd drive by and my father would always point to it from behind the wheel, "There's Froehmer's house." I even sat in the car, parked right out front, while my father went inside. I remember thinking how impressive the house was, how much bigger and better it seemed than our house. It seemed small now, and all I could think about was how I'd never been inside. I'd known Froehmer almost my entire life and I'd never set foot in his house, had never been invited. It didn't matter. Froehmer would get the trophy.

Maybe it was for himself, maybe he had a thing for them; maybe his whole house was full of stolen trophies. Or maybe it was for somebody else after all, a nothing piece of glory that had become its own sport, its own business. It had cost him. At least it cost him.

I walked to the back door and pounded on it as if I owned the place. Every knock was like a punch in my left shoulder. I kept knocking until I saw Froehmer make his way toward me. He didn't look happy. Maybe he knew what had happened already. I didn't care. I leaned against the door frame and when he opened the door, I handed him the black bag.

He opened it and his eyes lit up like a kid's at Christmas.

"I took it from Mobley," I told him. "He had it for someone else."

He didn't take his eyes off the thing. I had to get out of there.

"Where's Mobley now?"

"Dead." Froehmer's face didn't change. Not even a little. Not at all.

"But where is he?"

"I took care of it."

He looked up. "You need help," he said. "Let me call somebody."

"I just need some rest."

"You have a gun? If you have one, you better give it to me."

"I took care of it," I told him. "I took care of everything. And now you have it."

He put the trophy back in the bag.

"I did it for you," I told him. "I never . . . you never . . . all those years, you never told me you played," I said.

A spiteful contraction gradually distorted his face. "No one wants to hear about it," he said. "But I was better than most of them. They knew it. I was better than them. But that's history."

"What's it for then?"

"They owe it to me, so I take it from them," he said. "It's not for me. I'm setting the record straight." He looked at me, right in the eye. "You better go on now."

"And Frank? And Mobley? What about them?"

"You better go on," Froehmer said. "You need to take care."

"You have to answer about Mobley," I said. "How could you do that? All this time."

"We'll talk about that," he said. "We'll talk about Mobley. A hard man to replace, you know. But we'll take care of it. You'll be all right."

"I'm done," I said. I wanted to tell him that I was done with the stealing and done with the killing, but I couldn't say it right then. "We'll talk about it," he said and closed the door and I watched him carry the black bag with him.

I thought I might take the trophy from him, just to get that satisfied look off his face, just to remind him that it wasn't his, that he wasn't entitled to it, that having it didn't mean anything. If it's what mattered to him, I could show him that I could take it again and again, whenever I wanted.

I was going to kill Froehmer. He might try to get me first, or rather, have someone else come after me. Or he might continue on with me, the way he always had, continuing to use me for whatever he needed, however he needed it. Maybe he'd offer me Mobley's old spot. Isn't that how you got ahead in this fucked-up world? I'm sure Froehmer would have it figured out before I did. He had me in a box he thought I couldn't escape. Maybe I would go on the way I always did, doing whatever Froehmer told me to do. What else was I going to do? I didn't know where it was all going, or how long it would take. But I knew I would kill him.

I walked back toward the car up ahead. I could see Casey sitting in the passenger seat, waiting. Her silhouette, the dark outline of her head, for a second looked almost like Frank. It could have been any number of times, any number of jobs, with me walking back to the car, with

Frank waiting. How many times had it happened? How many times had I walked back with something under my arm, in my coat, in a bag? Nothing for us, but all of it going to Froehmer. Every single time. Everything for Froehmer.

But this time was different. This time, the last time, I wouldn't have anything. Nothing. This time I'd get in and he'd say, "What happened? You put it back?" I put it back. The way I would have if he had asked. I would have taken it back; I would have taken it back immediately. All he had to do was ask. Only he didn't. He decided he'd take it back. And now he wasn't waiting.

A car came up the street and I kept my eyes forward and the headlights lit up Casey's face. I got in the driver's seat and for the first time thought there was more blood than before. It seemed like it was everywhere.

"I think you better drive," I said.

Casey must have shot me by accident. A slug must have passed through Mobley and went into my shoulder. Or else a round ricocheted off the floor. It didn't matter how it got there; I had a bullet in me and I was going to have to get it out. I couldn't go to a hospital, but I couldn't go on much longer the way I was either. I pulled my jacket off the shoulder and felt for the spot. Blood was all over the place.

"Did I do that?" Casey said.

"No," I told her "Mobley. I think it's bad."

She pulled the shirt away from the wound and looked at it. She found a towel in the back seat and pressed it into the shoulder. I held it there and she said, "It's not as bad as it looks. I'll take care of it. We'll get home and I'll take care of it." I knew she would. There wasn't much in the world I could be sure of, but I was certain of that. It was enough. For now.

ACCOMPLICES AND EASY MARKS

Deb Aaronson, Michael Barson, A. I. Bezzerides ("chipped glass" *Thieves' Market*, 122; "The way they cook in this place" *On Dangerous Ground*, 213), Leigh Brackett ("a more dignified form of endeavour" *The Long Goodbye*, 219), Carl Bromley, Richard Brooks ("but afterwards, we'll have business together" *The Killers*, 214), W. R. Burnett ("Small-timers for small jobs" *High Sierra*, 6), Raymond Chandler ("the machinery had started to move and nothing could stop it" *Double Indemnity*, 158; "You can't figure them all" *Double Indemnity*, 241), G. K. Chesterton ("Thieves respect property" *The Man Who Was Thursday*, 169), Jim Collins, Charles Dickens ("got his own horse down to a straw a day . . ." *Oliver Twist*, 13), Fyodor Dostoyevsky ("I do not recognize any judgment over me, I know all the same that I will be judged" *The Idiot*, 162; "with one blow, like a sheep" *The Idiot*, 216), Marina Drukman, Daniel Fuchs ("jobs like that, one after another" *Criss Cross*, 89; "the way you know everything, the way you figure it all out" *Criss Cross*, 239), Jean Genet ("see omens in the slightest accidents" *The Thief's Journal*, 4), David Halpern, George V. Higgins ("I keep looking at you . . ." *Trust*, 178), John C. Higgins ("You're never slow sticking my neck out" *Border Incident*, 193), Patricia Highsmith ("This is what I like, sitting at a table and watching people go by. It does something to your outlook on life" *The Talented Mr. Ripley*, 74), John Huston ("but afterwards, we'll have business together" *The Killers*, 214), Peter Kranitz, Maurice Leblanc ("By what signs can one hope to identify a face" *The Confes-

sions of Arsène Lupin, 7), Michael Lindgren, Ross MacDonald ("it didn't look as if it had any money in it, or ever would again" *The Way Some People Die*, 194), Gina Maolucci, Herman Melville ("In general, a black and shameful period lies before me . . ." *The Confidence-Man*, 77), Melville House, Eddie Muller, Edmund H. North ("don't judge his brains by yours" *Colorado Territory*, 228), Janet Oshiro, Kazu Otsuka ("I'm not begging anyone" *Pigs and Battleships*, 193), Jo Pagano ("They sure drop the net over you, don't they?" *The Sound of Fury*, 21), Abraham Polonsky ("You worried about it . . ." *Odds Against Tomorrow*, 62; "just to live and be guilty" *Force of Evil*, 225), Nicholas Ray ("The way they cook in this place" *On Dangerous Ground*, 213), Alain Robbe-Grillet ("A spiteful contraction gradually contorted his face" *The Erasers*, 244), The Robbins Office, Martin Scorsese ("if I do something wrong I want to pay for it in my own way" *Mean Streets*, 126), Georges Simenon ("He was almost a mascot, like a family pet you are used to seeing in the same place" *Dirty Snow*, 113), Ross Thomas (185), B. Traven ("Don't play innocent; you know what we want" *The Treasure of the Sierra Madre*, 193), John Twist ("don't judge his brains by yours" *Colorado Territory*, 228), Antony Veiller ("but afterwards, we'll have business together" *The Killers*, 214), Billy Wilder (the machinery had started to move and nothing could stop it" *Double Indemnity*, 158; "You can't figure them all" *Double Indemnity*, 241), Mary Wowk.